Kids For Sail

Pamela & Sam Bendall

Orca Book Publishers

Canadian Cataloguing in Publication Data
Bendall, Pamela,
   Kids for sail

   ISBN 0-920501-49-4
   1. Yachts and yachting — Pacific Ocean.
2. Sailing — Pacific Ocean. 3. Children —
Travel — Pacific Ocean. 4. Kluane II (Yacht).
5. Bendall, Sam, 1977- 6. Bendall, Charlie.
GV817.P23B45 1990   910'.916404   C90-091482-3

Publication assistance provided by the Canada Council.

We gratefully acknowledge the financial support of the
Government of British Columbia.

Orca Book Publishers
P.O. Box 5626, Stn. B.
Victoria, B.C. Canada
V8R 6S4

Design by Christine Toller.
Typeset by Grafix Publishing and Design
Printed and bound in Canada.

To our dedicated skipper, Michael, who had the courage to turn our dream into reality, together with the necessary sailing skills to meet every challenge and bring us all home safely.

The authors of this book are grateful to all our friends and relatives for their support and encouragement throughout our voyage and during the writing of *Kids for Sail*.

Special thanks to Dennis and Diane Fedoruk, Jeanne Harvey and Brian Johnson for loyally looking after our affairs during our two-and-a-half-year absence from Canada. We would also like to recognize Rem Van Stalk and Meaghan Byers for their assistance as crew on various sections of our journey. Although their participation in the adventure has been omitted from the storyline, we cannot overlook their contribution.

Finally, *Kids for Sail* would not have been possible without the dedication of two people: our editor Ann Featherstone, who applied exceptional ability and diligence towards making this book special; and our publisher Bob Tyrrell, who believed in us and gave us the opportunity to become authors.

1.   Kids for Sail

Sam thought it was going to be an ordinary morning when he pulled on his clothes and got ready for school. It looked like any other November morning: dull and grey, with a hint of snow in the clouds. But when he went downstairs for breakfast, he knew right away that something was different. Mom and Dad had very serious expressions on their faces — the kind that said they meant business. Charlie, Sam's younger brother, looked unconcerned as he sat at the table with his nose in a glass of orange juice. As usual, whenever there was any food around, it had Charlie's undivided attention. Nothing, but nothing, distracted Charlie from his mission to search and destroy every last bit of food on his plate.

Sam's father leaned against the counter with his arms crossed: a bad sign. Usually, Dad's head was buried in the newspaper first thing every morning. Sam racked his brains as he sat down in front of the bowl of porridge that Mom was dishing out. What had he done? It could be any number of things, of course. The mess in his room, his habit of sleeping as late as he possibly could, the fight he had picked with Charlie yesterday. Sam was just opening up his mouth to apologize for whatever it was, when his mom sat down in her chair and smiled.

"Boys, your dad and I have something important to tell you. We have decided to move."

"Move?" Sam's jaw dropped a foot. Even Charlie looked up from his cereal. "What? Do you . . . do you mean leave Whitehorse?" Sam sputtered.

"That's right," she answered. "We're going to sell the house, our furniture, the cars, even most of your toys, I'm afraid."

"What?" Charlie dropped his spoon at the mention of toys. Sam, at nine, was too old to care about toys that much, but Charlie wasn't even four yet.

"You can take a few things, like your Lego blocks, but there just won't be much room where we are going," Dad offered. "You see, our new home is only forty feet long. Her name is *Kluane* (he pronounced it clue-on-knee), and she is a sailboat."

"What?" This time, both Sam and his brother cried out in unison. They were crazy, Sam thought. Mom and Dad were absolutely crazy. Charlie and Sam had both been born and raised in Whitehorse. They had never lived even near the ocean. And now they were going to live *on* the ocean?

"She's a beautiful boat," Mom explained patiently. "A Beneteau First 38, made in France. Wait till you see her. You know your father has always dreamed of sailing around the Pacific Ocean." Both boys sat with their mouths open. "We've thought about this very carefully," she continued. "We'll all have to learn to become sailors. The trip will probably take three years and it will be a year before we get started. The boat is moored in Victoria and we'll have to prepare her for the trip."

Then Sam began to think. He'd have to say goodbye to all his friends — that would be sad. But no more long, cold winters — that would be all right. And if they were always on a boat, then maybe they wouldn't have . . . a magic hope seized him.

"Does this mean," he spoke up, "no more school?"

"We will be your teachers," explained his mom. "We have already registered you in grade five and Charlie in kindergarten. You will both be studying by correspondence. And while we are in Victoria, Sam, you'll go to a school called Glenlyon."

So much for that dream, Sam thought, shrugging his shoulders and pulling a long face. But his parents ignored him. Taking a map out of the kitchen drawer, his father spread it out over the table, on top of their breakfast, bowls, glasses and everything.

"Now look," he said, tracing the route with his finger, "here's the Pacific Ocean. We're going to Hawaii, then down here to the Line Islands, Samoa, Tonga, Fiji, then all the way to New Zealand. Did you know that there are over 30,000 islands in the Pacific? It's the largest ocean in the world. And oceans cover seventy-one percent of the surface of the earth."

"I wonder why they don't call it 'Planet Ocean,'" Sam broke in, suddenly very excited. He stared at the huge area of blue on the table. "Hey, this is really neat! We're really going to do this!"

His mom laughed. "You bet we are, Sammy."

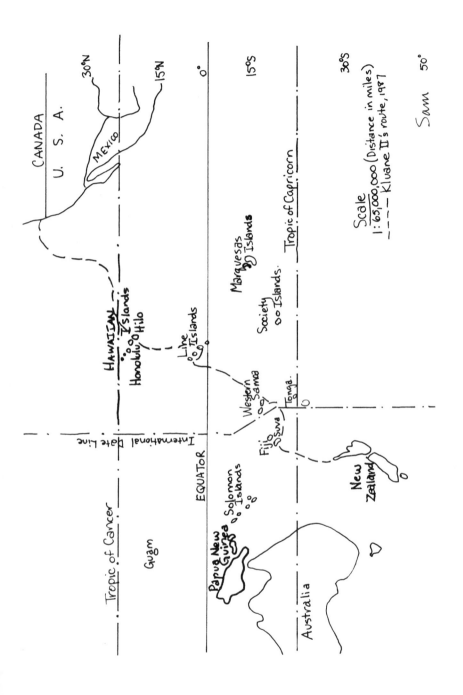

CANADA

U. S. A.

Mexico

30°N

15°N

0°

15°S

Tropic of Capricorn

30°S

Sam 50°

Scale
1:65,000,000 (Distance in miles)
--- Kluane II's route, 1987

HAWAIIAN Islands
Honolulu ○ Hilo

Line
○ ○ Islands

Marquesas
◯◯ Islands

Society
○○ Islands

International Date Line

Western
Samoa ○○

Tonga ◯

Fiji ○ Suva

EQUATOR

Tropic of Cancer

Guam

Papua New
Guinea

Solomon
Islands ○○

New
Zealand ◯

Australia

2. Hawaii, Here We Come!

May 24
Dear Diary,

My friend Tristan gave me this diary yesterday when they had a going away party for me at Glenlyon School. I was only there one year, but I sure made a lot of good friends, and I know I'm going to miss them. The whole class came down to the boat to say good-bye, and after each classmate took a guided tour through Kluane II, we toasted to the trip with ice cream cones. Since Kluane doesn't have a freezer, that ice cream cone will be my last one for a while.

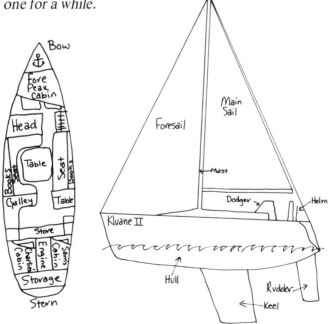

Sam put his pencil down and looked around his new room. No, "cabin" was the right word for it, he reminded himself. He would have to get used to all the sailing expressions he had learned over the last year. He was in the aft cabin in the stern of *Kluane* — in other words, the back of the boat. The "bow" was the front, left was "port" and right was "starboard." Why didn't people just say left or right, front or back? No one could answer that question to Sam's satisfaction. Even Mom and Dad had new titles. Dad was the "skipper" and Mom was the "first mate" now. He and Charlie were "crew."

If he stretched just a little in his bunk, his feet could hang over the end. This wasn't like his room at home. Sam's dresser and desk were no bigger than his locker and desk at Glenlyon School. There were loads of books in the main cabin, as well as plenty of art supplies to keep him entertained, but his own cabin was pretty basic. A small bookshelf above his desk, his bunk, which also served as a chair, and a tiny dresser. That was it. His cabin also doubled as a storage room, where tins of canned meat and fish shared space on the shelf with his few personal possessions. Just as well, Sam grimaced. It would be easier to keep tidy. He had been known as "the sloth" in the past (he'd rather hang around than tidy up his room), but all that would have to change, Mom warned him. Everything — clothes, papers, books, etc. — had to be kept stored carefully in case *Kluane* hit a big wave.

"Sam, Charlie, come on up," his dad called from the helm. "Last chance to see land."

Sam hopped off his bunk, shot out of his cabin and scrambled over Charlie, who was somersaulting his way through the tiny corridor. Dad was at the helm, eyes on the waves beginning to build ahead of them. Charlie called the helm a steering wheel, and it really did look like an enormous steering wheel, especially when Charlie gave it a try. He had to look through the spokes, as the top of the wheel was above his head.

"Look behind me, fellas," Dad said, as Charlie followed Sam up the steps to the deck. The boys could still see land, but just barely. As the swells of the ocean grew higher and higher, the faint silhouette of land on the horizon became smaller and smaller. *Kluane* was pulling them away from Victoria and their home. Sam never thought it would actually happen, but at last they had left Canadian soil, and now they were heading out to sea. The past few weeks had been so busy — with final plans for the journey and good-bye parties with friends. There hadn't been time to stop and think about their new life and what it would mean to Sam and Charlie.

"It sure is quiet out here," Sam ventured.

"Better get used to it," Dad laughed. "Our next port is Hawaii, and that is at least three weeks away, or 2,450 nautical miles."

Charlie piped up, "What's a nautical mile?"

"You don't even know what a regular mile is," Sam said with just the right amount of contempt in his voice to suggest that, of course, *he* knew what a nautical mile was. But Sam hoped his dad would tell them, just the same.

"It's not much longer than an ordinary mile on land. In fact, it's 1.1 miles," Dad answered.

The sea ahead was dark, an angry blue-grey that was nothing like the colour of the water closer to shore. *Kluane II* was now riding the waves like a roller coaster, rocking sideways as she surfed down each wave.

"All right!" shouted Charlie. The cabin floor was now a perfect slide. And Charlie, future gymnast, was in his element, slipping and sliding sideways. Sam's little brother was already famous for somersaulting on the cabin handrails. All that energy had to be used up somehow.

It was Dad's forty-first birthday. Mom was attempting to

ice a cake with one hand as the other gripped the counter. Everything in the galley, except the stove, moved with the motion of the waves. But the stove and its cooktop surface had to remain horizontal, since boiling water (not to mention the bread in the oven) would be dangerous if it flew all over the cabin. So the oven was gimballed, which means that it was attached in such a way that it could pivot.

"Charlie, for heaven's sake, stop rolling around under my feet," Mom said in exasperation as she lifted a foot for the tenth time. "You're driving me crazy."

Sam had helped decorate the main cabin as they got under way. Dad was so busy on deck that he didn't even notice the growing jungle of streamers and balloons below. As *Kluane* pitched and tossed about, the decorations came alive, swaying back and forth in unison like they were keeping time to music. Sam gripped the galley rail as he stared, transfixed by the sight.

At first all that pitching about had been fun. But now he was beginning to feel a little queasy. Were the waves just going to get higher and higher until the family reached Hawaii? Even Charlie had stopped tumbling and was crouched on the steps to the deck, his face turning a pea-soup green. Sam wondered if his own face was taking on such a becoming colour.

"Mom," Charlie called suddenly, "Dad's being sick over the side!"

Whenever there was an emergency, Sam would watch his mom's face. Hardly anything bothered her, so if she looked worried, then he knew they were really in trouble. Sam turned anxiously to watch her reaction. She didn't look worried. In fact she had a smile on her face as she flew past Sam and pulled the video camera out of a storage compartment in the main cabin.

"Are you having a happy birthday?" Sam heard Mom

call, when she trained the camera on Dad. Sam's dad lifted his head from over the side.

"You are a cruel woman, Pamela," he groaned.

Soon both Sam and Charlie began to feel sick to their stomachs as well. No one even went near the birthday cake that night.

It was frustrating. Sam had learned so much about sailing and wanted to help Dad, but all he could do was lie down in the main cabin and try to settle his stomach. *Kluane* continued to ride the roller coaster of waves. Nobody was smiling now. Sam wondered if Dad was having second thoughts about his lifetime dream; this was definitely not Sam's idea of a good time.

Suddenly he was overwhelmed by nausea. "Mom," Sam cried, "over here!" Mom came running with the bucket, but it was too late. He was sick all over the cabin floor.

Just as she was mopping up Sam's mess, Charlie called with the same urgency, "Mom, I'm going to be sick!"

For the rest of the day, Mom ran back and forth between both of them with the bucket and cleaned up the floor if she couldn't get there fast enough.

May 25
Dear Diary,

I can't tell you how awful this last 24 hours has been. Everyone is seasick except Mom. We are all really miserable because Kluane is knocking about all over the place so we can barely stand up. I have to hold on to the boat all the time — even when I'm sleeping. They gave me seasick medicine, which helps a bit, but it makes me really tired.

"In fact," he mumbled as he gripped the side of his bunk, "I'm too tired to even write." Just keeping still in his bunk was an effort. Sam knew he should be helping Dad and Mom sail the boat, but he felt so sick, he just wanted to lie in his cabin. Because Dad was a doctor, he had several types of medicines to help with seasickness. But none of them had worked so far. Dad finally tried a new type of medicine — patches that were placed on the skin behind the ears. The medicine in the patch was supposed to be absorbed into the body through the skin. Maybe they would make a difference.

Yesterday, Sam had been sick more times than he could count. Often he couldn't get outside in time. Making a trip on deck meant putting on special vests that hooked onto lines running all around *Kluane*. There was never time to do that. Just as Mom would be holding the bucket for one of them, the other one would be sick too.

Sam rolled off his bunk and groped his way into the main cabin, where Charlie was curled up on one of the seats. Mom was cleaning the cabin floor again. She used salt water for cleaning because the fresh-water tanks held only 120 gallons, which was just enough to last them until Hawaii.

"Mom," Sam asked sleepily, "Dad said the ocean accounts for ninety-seven percent of the world's water supply. So if there's so much water around *Kluane*, why can't we just drink the salt water instead of fresh?"

"Because it's not healthy to consume too much salt. We could die very quickly if we ran out of fresh water," she explained. "*Kluane* is equipped with systems for collecting fresh rainwater, and we are always watching the clouds in case a downpour is approaching so that everyone can have fresh-water showers on the boat deck. This way we can save whatever fresh water we do have for drinking and emergencies."

Both boys were quiet for the moment so Mom took a break, sitting back on the seat between them. "Ocean currents are

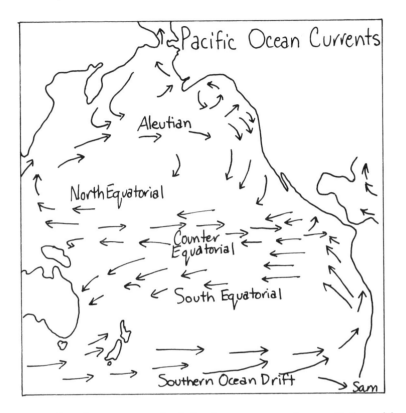

caused by the amount of salt in the water, you know," she said. "Cold water is denser than warm water."

"Do you mean dumber?" Charlie yawned.

"No," Mom laughed. "That means it has more salt in it and is heavier. Cold water from the North and South Poles flows along the ocean floor back to the equator, causing undercurrents beneath the warmer water from the tropics. This continuous exchange of cold and warm water is one reason currents exist. Prevailing winds are also responsible for making currents as well as land formations at the water surface and along the ocean floor. I had to learn all of this to become a sailor," she added, "because currents can have an effect on the direction we take just as much as the weather does. You'll be learning a lot of this soon, Sammy."

May 27
Dear Diary,
   Sick today.

Two days later the sea was still rolling. People had warned
Sam about seasickness, but somehow he never imagined it could
be this awful. The motion had made it difficult to move around
the boat comfortably for the past three days, so it was impossible
to do anything. Sam discovered that if he sat outside on deck, he
didn't feel quite so sick. But sometimes the weather was so rough
that it was too dangerous to go outside. Huge swells often
crashed right over *Kluane*, strong enough to knock them right
over.

Everyone on *Kluane* had to tie themselves to the boat by
wearing the harness with a clip attached. Strong lines ran along
both sides of *Kluane*, so with one clip of the safety line, they
could walk the length of the boat.

There was nothing to be afraid of, Sam reminded himself.
Kluane had loads of safety equipment, including a six-man life
raft that would pop open if the boat began to sink. And the raft
was full of emergency rations (that was what Dad called food).
They also had self-releasing fire extinguishers, emergency
distress signals, and a satellite navigation system so they knew
exactly where they were at all times.

Sam and Charlie spent most of the day in the main cabin,
watching Mom struggle to keep the boat tidy and prepare meals
for the family in the tiny galley. It was lucky that she didn't get
seasick, or they would have been in real trouble, Sam realized.

Making soup was a real challenge, but Mom seemed
determined to try. *Kluane* rocked about so much, she had to grab
the counter with one hand while she worked. Just as she opened

the spice cupboard, a huge wave crashed against the hull, and all twenty-two spice bottles came flying out of the cupboard in twenty-two different directions. They landed everywhere. Charlie whooped with delight, then covered his mouth when he saw Sam's warning stare. But it was pretty funny, Sam admitted to himself, watching Mom scramble around the cabin after the rolling spices. Just as she would reach a spice bottle, another wave would hit *Kluane*, sending the bottle flying in another direction.

"It's important to keep a sense of humour," she muttered between clenched teeth.

Even though Sam knew how difficult it was to make the soup, he secretly hoped that Mom would succeed, because for the first time since they left Canada, he finally felt hungry.

May 29
Dear Diary,

I'm writing to you now because I may not get another chance for a while. Dark clouds like I've never seen before are coming in fast. I know Dad is worried because all the sails have been reefed — that means made smaller. He keeps listening to our Sony shortwave radio for weather reports.

3.   Gale

"Close the hatches!" shouted Dad. "Pamela, I need you on deck."

Sam jumped off his bunk, reaching his door just as Mom flew past and stumbled up the steps to the helm.

"Michael," she called, "the weather report predicts gale force winds, heavy thunder and lightning. They think the gale will last another twenty-four hours at least."

Her voice had an edge to it that Sam didn't like. She sounded calm, but the kind of calm that could turn into panic any second.

"Mom," he called uncertainly, "how much is gale force?" But Mom didn't answer him. She was too busy attaching her safety lines over her wet weather gear. This was no time for a polite conversation.

Sam retreated to the main cabin and pulled one of the sailing books down off the shelf. He remembered Dad talking about the Beaufort Wind Scale. There had to be something in there about it. Sam flipped through the pages until he found a chart marked "Beaufort Scale." Under the section called "description," he saw the word "gale." He looked at the column next to it.

"Waves greater height. Foam blown into streaks," he said aloud. "That means the wind is between thirty-four and forty knots. That doesn't sound too bad."

He climbed up onto the seat and peered at the porthole. Through the salt-streaked glass he could just make out the waves

Beaufort Wind Scale

Wind Speed	Description	Effects at Sea	Effects on Land
Knots under 1	Calm	Like a mirror	Calm, smoke rises straight
1 - 3	Light air	Ripples	Smoke indicates wind direction
4 - 6	Light breeze	Small wavelets	Wind felt on face
7 - 10	Gentle breeze	Large wavelets	Light flags extend
11 - 16	Moderate breeze	Small waves Numerous whitecaps	Small branches move
17 - 21	Fresh breeze	Many whitecaps Small spray	Small trees spray
22 - 27	Strong breeze	Larger waves Whitecaps everywhere	Large branches move Whistling heard in wires
28 - 33	Near gale	White foam from breaking waves. Waves 4 - 6 metres	Whole trees in motion Resistance when walking
34 - 40	Gale	Waves greater height Foam blown into streaks	Twigs and small branches break off trees
41 - 47	Strong gale	High waves of 6 metres Spray reduces visibility	Slight structural damage in houses
48 - 55	Storm	Very high waves 6 - 9 metres Sea white and rolling	Trees broken, uprooted Seldom seen on land
56 - 63	Violent storm	Waves 9 - 14 metres Visibility reduced, sea white	Widespread damage Rarely experienced
64 plus	Hurricane	Air filled with foam Sea white, visibility greatly reduced	Widespread damage Rarely experienced

near the boat. They looked pretty high, but how could he tell if they were a "greater height?" And how could he tell if the foam out there was a "streak" or not? Sam scrambled down again and grabbed the book. "Spray reduces visibility. That sounds pretty close," he muttered. Then his finger followed the description to the next column. "Strong gale," he read, "Forty-one to forty-seven knots." The next line below said "Storm."

"Whew," he said, putting the book aside.

Sam looked up. He'd better make sure Charlie was prepared for this. Mom and Dad would be busy on deck, and they didn't need any kids in the way. He had to take care of his brother. Suddenly Sam felt grown up as he worked his way back to Charlie's cabin.

During the day, it had been pretty easy to keep Charlie distracted, but once the dim light of that afternoon finally deserted them, Sam's show of bravery was beginning to wear a little thin. The wind was howling so loudly that they could barely hear themselves think, let alone hear each other talk.

Only once did Mom work her way through the cabin to check on the boys. "Sammy," she said tersely, "you'll have to make us some sandwiches and coffee, if you can manage it. Your dad and I will probably stay on deck all night." She smiled down at Charlie, who was as white-faced and quiet as they had ever seen him. "It's all right, Char Char," she added. "We just have to keep an eye on the sails and keep *Kluane* steered into the waves. Everything will be fine. You boys will have to sleep here tonight. Sam, you know how to put up the lee cloth so you are tied into these bunks. You'd be flying around too much in your own cabins." And then she was gone, gripping the rails and door frames as she headed back to the deck.

Sam did as he was told, and the boys had a strangely quiet dinner, one hand holding their sandwiches while the other held the table edge firmly. It took all their concentration just to eat. When they cleaned up as best they could, Sam helped Charlie into his sleeping bag and attached the lee cloth, which formed a wedge of canvas between the top and bottom of the bunk.

"There you go, you hairy little caterpillar," he said to Charlie, before turning to his bunk. Normally, remarks like that would have resulted in howls of protest, and appeals to Mom ("Mom, Sam called me a caterpillar!"). But not tonight. Charlie smiled politely and squirmed down into his sleeping bag.

Sam repeated the routine with his own bunk and crawled as deeply as he could into his sleeping bag. But even the lee cloth couldn't keep him from rocking back and forth with the motion of *Kluane*. Even when he put his head under his pillow, the crashing of the boat was too furious to allow sleep. "I hope it goes away soon," he muttered. Sam tried to concentrate on the sight of his brother, who was rolling around in his own cocoon.

Despite the strong winds and frantic seas, Charlie eventually fell asleep, his hunched figure as still as the motion of the boat would allow. But Sam lay awake for what seemed like hours, imagining his parents working above. They would be continuously adjusting *Kluane*'s sails to ensure that the boat was safe. He knew how important it was to keep control of the boat and steer it on the proper course. The strong seas and high winds could easily knock *Kluane* over if they weren't careful. Sam could see them dressed in their protective rain gear and their strong safety harnesses. When a huge wave crashed over the boat and flung Sam against the lee cloth, he imagined Mom and Dad covered in spray while they worked even harder to keep *Kluane* on course.

"Way to go, Mom and Dad," he murmured. They'd take care of everything. They knew what to do. They'd take care . . .

"Sam, Sammy are you all right? Are you okay, honey?"

Sam lifted his head groggily. What was he doing on the floor under the table? he wondered. "Yeah I'm fine," he answered in a daze, then he crawled back into his sleeping bag.

A giant wave had struck against the side of the hull, knocking *Kluane* totally out of control, breaking Sam's lee cloth, and throwing him across the cabin. Confused but too exhausted to care, Sam was back in his bunk and asleep before his mom had fixed the lee cloth once more.

The gale lasted for another full day. Mom and Dad hadn't slept at all, but they continued to work. Eventually both Sam and Charlie became brave enough to venture outside, where they could really see the awesome power of the waves. But *Kluane* plowed right on through, in spite of everything. By the end of the day, Sam's confidence in the boat's endurance was restored.

The next morning, as Sam was just about to climb out of his sleeping bag, he noticed something horribly strange happening to his eyesight. He couldn't focus clearly on anything. The entire cabin was a blur.

"Dad!" he screamed. "Help me quickly. I'm going blind!"

Dad raced down the steps into the cabin and found Sam bravely trying to hold back his tears.

"Everything is blurry. I can't even see my hands!" he cried.

"Did you touch that medicine patch behind your ears?" Dad asked.

"I'm not sure. Maybe I did, because it's getting awfully itchy."

"It can cause temporary blurriness to your vision, Son. I'm really sorry to say that it could be a few days before you'll be able to see properly again. You have to be brave and bear with it because there's nothing I can do to help. Maybe it's best that we take those patches off now, especially if they're itchy." Dad gave him a big hug for bravery and then removed the medicine patches.

Soon after that, Mom lost her sight as well. Because her contact lenses absorbed the medicine, they were ruined and had to be thrown out. Dad decided that they would never use those patches again, even if they did help lessen the seasickness a bit.

June 6

Dear Diary,

I know it has been a long time since I wrote to you but I couldn't see for almost a week. Boy, I hope I never go through that again! Luckily the problem only lasted a week, and it wasn't permanent. So, now I'll try to remember all the things that have happened lately.

The best news is that Charlie now has a friend. He was getting very lonely before and driving me crazy. Now we have a pet albatross following us. Charlie has named him "Albert Trossie." He does wonderful tricks in flight, especially for food, so we throw him all our edible garbage.

Charlie and I looked up "albatross" in our bird book. We discovered that these birds can live a long time at sea and are well known to oceangoing vessels. Albatrosses need strong air currents to fly and have incredibly long wings. They have been found as far away as 3,200 kilometers from their babies — that's as far away as the distance between Whitehorse and Vancouver!

The book also says that they nest on land in shallow grooves of mud or soil. Both the males and females incubate and feed their young. Albatrosses convert food that they eat into an oily substance in their stomachs so that it can be stored without deterioration for long periods of time. Yuck! When albatrosses choose their mates, they do a spectacular courtship dance in flight and stay with that mate for life.

So I guess that's why Charlie spends his entire day on deck with Albert Trossie. Albert's chosen Charlie!

That afternoon the boys began serious preparations for the halfway party. While Mom got to work in the galley, Charlie and Sam unrolled the streamers and blew up balloons. It seemed a little silly to be having a party in the middle of the ocean, but Sam didn't care. They needed a change.

Finally, at four o'clock, Dad shouted from the helm, "That's it! We've passed the halfway mark. We're halfway to Hawaii."

Charlie was first up the steps, followed by Sam. The sea had finally calmed enough to allow everyone to balance easily. Sam tied a balloon onto "Hans," the self-steering device, while Charlie stared anxiously around him. Nothing looked that different, Sam had to admit, as his eyes followed his younger brother's gaze out to sea.

"Where's the marker, Dad?" Charlie asked. "I don't see anything."

Dad laughed, "There isn't exactly a stick in the ocean, Charlie. I'm going by my calculations. But, honestly, we are halfway there. I figured the average distance we cover in a day and applied that to the distance we have to cover."

"Oh." Charlie sounded disappointed, but his eyes lit up at the sight of Mom and a tray of Cokes.

"First we toast the halfway mark of our trip, then you boys have to open your presents," she said.

Charlie couldn't believe all the wonderful things he was given. His six new gifts had two things in common: they were all small and could be used as new sources of entertainment on ocean passages. He got story tapes for his Walkman, art supplies, books, and new additions to his Lego collection. Sam got music tapes for the Walkman as well as art supplies and books. Dad received a present, too — a big supply of licorice — one taste they all really missed at sea.

Once the presents had been opened, they sat down to a huge feast of barbecued chicken, baked potatoes, carrots and fresh homemade bread. Sam knew Mom had worked all day preparing this meal. It was hard to believe that everything had come out of their tiny galley. The chocolate cake at the end of the meal was as good as Sam had ever tasted.

"Maybe," he said through his chocolaty grin, "this was worthwhile after all."

June 7
Dear Diary,

The weather has been so much calmer lately since we hit the trade winds about three days ago. Mom has been cooking super meals, and I can tell that Dad is more relaxed. The wind is now behind us, so Kluane *doesn't crash around like before. If all goes well, we will be in Hawaii in one more week. Fantastic! Hawaii, here we come!*

At last the trip was fun. The boys were finally beginning to participate in *Kluane*'s daily routine and learning the fundamentals of sailing. One morning, Dad announced that the boys would begin to take on "watch" rotations.

"Your Mom and I are getting exhausted, Sam," he explained. "We could really use an extra person on duty."

"I can too," Charlie protested. Dad was ready for him.

"Of course you'll be a great help too, Charlie," he replied quickly.

The person on "watch" had complete control of *Kluane*, so that others could sleep or relax. "Watch" was the perfect name for it, because that is exactly what Sam was told to do — watch out for everything. He learned to check the compass to see that they were on course, watch the clouds for signs of upcoming bad weather, and be sure no other boats or ships were coming towards the boat from any direction. Dad explained that most ships took an average time of fifteen minutes to reach the boat

CRUISING LOG BOOK

Date:	Time:	Course:	Speed:	Distance	Wind Speed / Direction	Barometer
30|6|87	0645 to 0845	187°T	6½ Knots	13 N.Miles	17 Knots Easterlies	1010

NOTES: *Nice beam reach, easy sailing. Saw excellent sunrise today. Tropic birds are all over here — must mean good fishing!* ☺ *Sam*

Satellite Navigator Fixes: 0715, 0750
Estimated Position: 15°N 155°W

from any point on the horizon. So the horizon had to be checked for traffic at least once every fifteen minutes throughout the entire twenty-four-hour day. No wonder Mom and Dad were so tired.

After his "watch," Sam recorded the data into the log book. He had to carefully calculate and record wind and boat speed, the distance they had travelled, temperature and barometer readings, plus anything else interesting, like ships passing or a school of fish jumping.

Charlie had a "watch" too — all fifteen minutes of it, Sam thought a little smugly. And even then, Charlie had to have a parent with him.

June 12
Dear Diary,

We're nearly there! I can't believe it. Ever since our three-quarter-way party, I haven't been able to think of anything else but Hawaii . . . icy cold Coke, ice cream, and a crisp red apple. Charlie keeps asking about going to the park — I think he needs to get rid of his energy. Mom is dreaming of soaking in a real bathtub, and I know all Dad wants is a good night's sleep.

The temperature is really warm now. Yesterday, Mom packed away all our winter clothes into storage. It's strange that only last week we were complaining of the cold, and now I hate to admit that it's almost too hot.

I hope we get there soon — these last three days are killing me!

June 14
Dear Diary,

I know we must be getting close because today I heard Radio Hawaii on my Walkman. Dad estimates that we should see land early tomorrow morning. I have nothing else to say but, I CAN'T WAIT!!!

But the next day they saw nothing. From different positions on the foredeck, Sam and Charlie squinted at the horizon, but no spot of land showed itself. When night fell, they sat up, too anxious to sleep. But the horizon was just as black as it had ever been.

Three hours went by before Sam began to really worry. He wouldn't say anything to his parents, but the fear of not being where they thought they were was starting to overwhelm him. There were still no signs of any lights from Hawaii, and he knew they should have seen it hours ago. No one spoke. Mom finally put Charlie to bed. Then the three of them sat motionless with their eyes fixed on the horizon.

Finally Sam could barely keep his eyes open, so he set his watch alarm for two hours and crawled into his bunk. When he awoke, there was still no sign of Hawaii. He quickly turned on his Walkman radio. To his relief Radio Hawaii was still very loud and clear. There still was some hope. By this time their charts showed *Kluane* forty miles from the Big Island, which Sam knew should easily have been close enough to see. Unless Hawaii was hidden by clouds, they were in trouble.

The thought of missing Hawaii after all this time was too depressing, so nobody spoke. Eventually a huge cloud appeared on the horizon straight in front of them. Hawaii had to be behind that cloud. With the exception of a few adjustments to the sails, no one moved for nearly two more hours. Sam finally decided that it was easier to pass the time sleeping than worrying. He found a spot beside his mom in the cockpit and faded into a deep sleep.

"There's a light!" yelled Dad, bringing Sam instantly alert.

"Yes, there's another one!" cried Mom.

Sam jumped up. By the time he had focused his eyes, the horizon was lined with brilliant lights. New ones kept appearing. It was so exciting that they all jumped and cheered. Charlie came out of his cabin, wondering what the commotion was all about. But when he saw the lights, he too joined in the celebration. *Kluane* was exactly where they had calculated her to be, with Hilo, on the Big Island of Hawaii, only a few hours away.

"I can't believe it . . . land!" cheered Sam.

4.   Hawaiian Birthday

June 15
Dear Diary,

 Dad just radioed Hawaii Customs so we can be cleared into the country. He explained our position and expected time of arrival. We can't set foot on American soil until we have been cleared through customs, so I hope they hurry. After exactly three weeks at sea, I'm not sure if I'll even be able to walk properly on land again.

 I think the arrival party is going to be the best party of all!

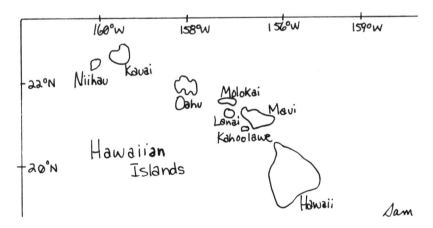

By morning, the clouds had cleared, and Hawaii's Big Island stood high above *Kluane*'s bow. They could even smell the land. After so long at sea, the scent of tropical vegetation seemed overpowering. Charlie was literally bouncing off the walls. Good thing the lifelines have nets attached to them, Sam thought, as Charlie scrambled up the steps to the deck for the twentieth time. Otherwise Charlie would have flung himself overboard by now.

"Sam! Sam! Look at this!"

Charlie was at the bow, hands on the railing as he jumped up and down madly. Sam effected a look of unconcern and casually followed his brother, but the sight that greeted him left him bouncing almost as high as Charlie.

"Wow!" he cried.

A huge school of dolphins was swimming alongside *Kluane* and crisscrossing in front of the bow. They seemed every bit as excited as the boys; their sleek grey bodies raced along and broke the surface of the water. Charlie was so entranced by the sight that he didn't notice Albert Trossie's absence, Sam suddenly realized. Albert had become a permanent fixture on deck, but the last time Sam had seen him was at sunset last night. No doubt Albert was as glad to see Hawaii as they were. He had just been hitching a ride.

When *Kluane* was finally ready to dock in Hilo, Sam ran on deck to help with the lines. Now that they had arrived, he felt like a real sailor. *Kluane* was just one of many boats docking this morning, and Hilo looked like any other port: overcrowded and very busy. Only the exotic flowers and palm trees in the distance reminded Sam that this wasn't Victoria.

The customs officer was the first person to greet *Kluane* when she was finally tied up. A big hearty man, he grasped each boy's hand and gave it a firm shake, then surveyed them both.

"You boys look like you need a good meal after that long trip," he said. "As soon as we finish signing these papers, I'm going to personally drive you to my favourite restaurant."

At that suggestion the boys whooped, threw themselves off the boat, and were halfway up the wharf when Mom called them back.

"Hold on you two," she called. "We're not going anywhere until the skipper and first mate have had their showers."

"Aw Mom," Sam moaned in frustration, as he and Charlie turned and shuffled back to *Kluane*.

It was a meal they would never forget. Sam ordered two large, icy cold Cokes from the smiling waitress.

"And I mean large, with lots of ice," he said, knowing that she would never understand why the drink was so important.

No one spoke as they gobbled down the foods they had craved most during the previous three weeks. Dad, Sam and Charlie had super-sized hamburgers with everything on them, followed by milkshakes and ice cream sundaes. Mom ordered the biggest salad on the menu, with a fruit salad for dessert. Only now did they really appreciate how little they had eaten while sailing.

When no one could manage another bite, the customs officer cheerfully drove them back to *Kluane*, adding a guided tour of all the spots they would need to find: laundry facilities, grocery stores, a hardware, and even a park where the boys could play.

Once they were back at *Kluane*, Dad turned and faced his crew.

"I order everyone to take the entire day off to do as they please," he said, with mock seriousness. Then he dismissed the company and disappeared into his cabin. Mom and Sam exchanged a knowing look. Dad would be out like a light for the rest of the afternoon.

Mom spent the first hour on the telephone, calling relatives and friends to let them know they were safe. Charlie and Sam played in the park next door to the marina. They tumbled in the grass, ran and ran, and then ran some more — just happy to be free from the confinement of *Kluane*.

Later at dinner, Sam decided to bring up an idea that was beginning to obsess him. It did seem like wishful thinking, but what the heck, he thought. His parents looked so relaxed.

"Hey Mom and Dad," he said casually, "since we're in Hawaii, and Hawaii is famous for it, do you think I could take up surfing? After all, my birthday is in twelve days, and I'd really love a surfboard for my birthday."

"Sam, that's really ridiculous," Dad answered. "We have enough problems finding space for things without adding a surfboard to our deck. Besides, we're on a tight budget now, so I should probably warn you that presents are going to be a lot smaller than what you're used to."

"I know Dad, but puleeeeese," Sam begged. But it was no use. The next thing he knew, Mom and Dad had pulled out some books, and the family had a lesson on volcanoes. Sam and Charlie looked at each other and grimaced. There was no understanding parents, especially theirs. This time Mom and Dad had really flipped out.

June 18
Dear Diary,

I think it's time I changed your name. After all, you've been my best companion on this trip so you really deserve a better name. I know, what would you think if I call you Tristan? That way I wouldn't miss my friend Tristan so much, and he did ask me to write to him every day.

Anyway, today we rented a car and drove to Kilauea National Park. This wasn't just an ordinary park but actually a live volcano site that you can drive and walk through. I felt like I was walking on the moon! Craters were bubbling madly and steam was soaring from the vents! Kilauea is Hawaii's newest and most active crater so it was kind of scary never knowing when it may erupt. The only thing I couldn't stand was the smell. Dad said it was the sulphur. It was just like rotten eggs—yuck!

We learned all about volcanoes today. I have to do projects on all the new things we learn throughout the trip plus make a scrapbook from our experiences. Tristan, it's as bad as school! When Mom makes me sit down and do work, I put on my school tie. It's the only part of my uniform I brought with me, but it reminds me of class. Let me tell you a few things I learned today so I don't forget.

About Volcanoes
by Sam Bendall

It's easier to understand volcanoes if you think that the earth's crust is made up of many large plates. These plates are called tectonic plates, and they move about very slowly. Scientists believe that the plates actually sit on a thick, dense mantle, which is about 2,900 kilometers deep and made of heavier rocks. The centre core of the earth is below the mantle and is supposed to be very hot and solid.

So as these plates move around, one plate may get forced down beneath another, one causing friction, pressure and heat, which melts the edge of the plate. The melted material is called magma. A volcano happens when the heat and pressure builds up so much that it bursts through the crust, and the hot magma from the earth's interior gets vented.

Most volcanoes are created from the tectonic plate action, but the Hawaiian Islands were formed by a special type of volcano. "Hot spots" in the mantle, lying far from the plate edge, have created a chain of eruptions, leaving new islands in the middle of the ocean floor. On Planet Earth there are approximately five hundred active volcanoes, and about twenty of them are in eruption in any one year.

Mom, Dad, Charlie, and I walked all through the park after our tour, but we couldn't get too close to the bubbling vents because of the smell and the heat. It really was an interesting day after all. I might decide to be a geologist when I grow up.

Sam chewed on the end of his pencil. Should he tell Tristan what happened next?

Getting back to *Kluane* hadn't been nearly as much fun. Dad and the boys stayed on deck while Mom went below to start dinner.

"Michael, can you come here for a second," she called almost immediately. The boys followed their dad into the main cabin where Mom was standing with a look of puzzlement on her face. Sam wrinkled his nose in disgust. There it was again, the smell of volcanoes!

"There must be a broken egg inside the storage locker," Dad suggested. Together, they opened the locker under the bunk and looked inside.

Suddenly, Mom shrieked. Before Sam knew it, she ran up the stairs and off the boat so fast, he thought she was flying. Sam and Charlie crowded over Dad's shoulder to have a look. There, under the bunk where Sam slept at sea, the entire floor was covered in white crawling maggots. The smell was overpowering.

"Oh gross!" Charlie shouted.

The boys made a fast exit for the beach, leaving the skipper alone with his boat.

Even after Dad had cleaned up the mess, Mom refused to go back on board until the smell was gone, so they all went out for dinner that night. By the time they returned to *Kluane*, she was at last free of the rotten-eggs smell.

Sam pulled at the knot in his tie as he looked down at the page. Should he tell Tristan? It *was* pretty disgusting. In fact, it was really gross. After only a second of hesitation, Sam bent over the table and began to write furiously again.

Five days later, the family left the Big Island and sailed into a few quiet anchorages before coming into Honolulu. Honolulu is a huge commercial city, so Mom and Dad planned to spend the next week stocking *Kluane* with provisions for the next six months. After Hawaii they wouldn't be in a large city again until they reached New Zealand. Mom and Dad had to make sure that there was enough food, medical supplies, spare parts, and anything else they might need.

Once in Honolulu, *Kluane* moored at the Hawaii Yacht Club, which was next to a beautiful beach. Sam and Charlie spent most of their day exploring the shoreline. They soon discovered that, in order to find a place to sit down, they had to arrive almost before sunrise each morning. The boys had never seen so many people crammed into one place. They could hardly see the sand. But looking out to sea was a different matter. Relatively few people braved the surf as they performed for the crowds of tanning people.

That's where I want to be, Sam thought enviously. If only I could talk Dad into coming here one day, maybe he'd buy me a surfboard. But it wouldn't be easy. Mom and Dad were so busy getting provisions, he'd be lucky to get any kind of birthday present, let alone a surfboard.

One morning, Sam gave it a try anyway.

"Hey Dad," he began, "I know you're really busy, but I think you should come over to the beach one day. I know how you like to 'people watch,' and there's more opportunity there than I've ever seen. Can you just spare a few minutes today?"

The answer surprised him. "Sure, Son. Right after lunch. How's that?"

So Sam spent the entire morning in his favourite spot, watching the surfers and dreaming of being there himself. After lunch, Sam and his dad wandered over to the beach, but it was so hot they couldn't stay too long. When Sam tried to point out the surfers, Dad kept getting distracted by all the good looking people walking by. Sam realized then that there was no hope. He'd never have a surfboard.

June 28
Dear Tristan,

This is the best birthday I've ever had! I woke up really early this morning to the smell of cake in the oven. Ten! I'm finally into double numbers.

Once everyone was awake, I opened my presents and got lots of new art supplies, books, and some small beach toys. So Charlie and I took off early for the beach. I have to admit, I was a little disappointed that I didn't get my surfboard.

Anyway, after lunch we went back to our favourite beach spot where I love to sit and watch the surfers. Charlie likes to play in the sand, so my new toys made him pretty happy.

I was kind of daydreaming, I guess, but suddenly something strange caught my eye on the water. An old lady was out there trying to ride the waves on a surfboard. She looked really ridiculous. She kept losing her balance and crashing into shore, totally out of control. But pretty soon I noticed that the bathing suit on this old lady was the same as Mom's. Can you believe it? It was Mom! You can't imagine how embarrassing it is to have your mom out there on a surfboard.

So I went to tell her about how silly she looked, when I learned that the board she was using was my birthday present! Mom explained that it's actually called a boogie board. It's smaller than an actual surfboard, so it's easier to learn on and won't take up as much space on Kluane.

So I spent the rest of the day practising, and it sure isn't as easy as it looks. I really love my board and can't wait for tomorrow so I can go surfing again.

June 30
Dear Tristan,

You should see me surf now. I'm not as good as the rest of the surfers here, but I'm much better than two days ago. It's too bad that we're leaving tomorrow, because I was just starting to get into it. Let's hope that the next port has a good surf.

You wouldn't believe Kluane. Every cabinet and locker is full with provisions. I think she's going to burst. Mom showed me the list of goods we have stored — here it is (you won't believe it!):

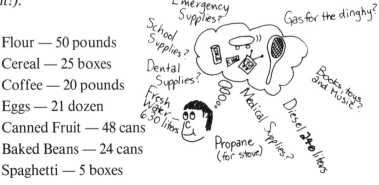

Flour — 50 pounds
Cereal — 25 boxes
Coffee — 20 pounds
Eggs — 21 dozen
Canned Fruit — 48 cans
Baked Beans — 24 cans
Spaghetti — 5 boxes

Milk — 48 liters
Powdered Milk — 2 boxes
Jam — 4 jars
Meat — 48 home-canned
Peanut Butter — 6 big jars
Juice — 48 litres
Rice — 10 pounds
Soup — 20 cans
Granola Bars — 200 bars
Vegetables — 20 jars home-canned
Aluminum Foil — 10 rolls
Toilet Paper — 100 rolls
Paper Towels — 50 rolls
Toothpaste — 10 tubes

Can you imagine storing all this stuff?

I wish we weren't leaving Hawaii because I really love it here. Our next port of call is a tiny little island named Fanning Island, about 1,300 nautical miles south of here. Dad says it should take about eight days to get there if the weather cooperates . . . I've heard that one before.

5. Lost at Sea

On July 1, *Kluane* sailed away from Hawaii under perfect conditions and clear skies. Everything, including Sam's new "boogie board," had been carefully stowed away so that nothing could fly about in rough seas. Sam was just beginning to notice a touch of seasickness appear again when his dad called him and Charlie to the navigation table.

"You both did so well with learning your watch and sailing skills last passage; how would you like to learn about navigation?"

"You mean I can learn how to press all those buttons?" Charlie asked, referring to the satellite navigator.

"No," replied Dad in a tone that meant they may not have any fingers left if they ever touch those buttons. "First, you have to understand the basics. We'll start by learning the 'dead reckoning' method of navigation. You'll each need a large sheet of paper, and the atlas."

"Couldn't they have thought of a better name for this navigation system than 'dead reckoning'?" Sam asked. But his father was too preoccupied to consider the question.

First they drew a map of the Pacific Ocean using reference lines of longitude (lines that run vertically on a map) and latitude (lines running horizontally on a map), with the equator lying right in the centre. The lines of latitude were numbered depending on where they lay in relation to the equator, which was 0.

"Canada is on the 49th parallel," Dad said, indicating the line bordering most of Canada and the United States, "which really means we are 49 degrees north of the equator, in the Northern Hemisphere. When *Kluane* crosses the equator, she'll be in the Southern Hemisphere and all of our latitude positions will be such-and-such degrees south.

"Longitude lines begin at 0 in Greenwich, England, and run east and west to 180 degrees. *Kluane* will be crossing the 180 degree mark when we sail through Tonga next month. By using these reference lines, we can properly place all the islands in the Pacific."

Dad next pulled a chart from the chart table and spread it out in front of the boys. The lines were there just like the lines they had drawn on their map.

"Seamen who navigate by water use charts instead of ordinary maps," he continued. "Just as road maps contain necessary information for people driving cars on land, nautical charts display important details for mariners. As *Kluane* progresses from one spot to another, her position is always recorded on the chart in order to avoid dangers and to find our destination."

Then Dad showed them how to use a ruler and compass to calculate their route and estimate the heading for the trip. Sam drew a line from their present position to the place where they wanted to end up, and used a special compass guide on the chart to find the compass bearing. Dad explained that other factors such as currents and wind direction had to be taken into account before they could make a final plan, which would then be written in the Log Book for reference. It didn't seem too complicated to Sam, although he wasn't sure if Charlie had any idea what was going on.

Sam's calculations showed *Kluane*'s position as 5 degrees

north and 150 degrees west. He compared it to the printout on the Satellite Navigator (called the "Sat Nav") and found it was right on!

"Good," said Dad, patting Sam on the back. "Now you're ready for Sat Nav. It receives a signal from passing satellites in the sky. This position of longitude and latitude is called a 'fix,' and it is relayed onto the screen. Every time *Kluane* gets a new fix, the machine beeps to let everyone know."

From then on, every time they heard a beep, Charlie and Sam would drop whatever they were doing and run to the navigation table. The skipper allowed Sam to record the fix on the chart, as long as he or Mom was supervising.

July 3
Dear Tristan,

Remember when I told you about those beeps from the Sat Nav? For the last couple of days Charlie and I have been constantly hearing beeps and running to the machine. Well, I don't know if Charlie or anyone else realizes it yet, but we haven't had a fix for five hours, and we usually get one at least every hour or so. I guess I shouldn't worry, but it's hard not to.

Later that night, Sam lay awake, too worried to sleep. He wished Dad hadn't taught him about the Satellite Navigator, because now he was certain something was terribly wrong. If the Sat Nav couldn't give them a fix, how would they know how to find the island? The murmur of his parents' voices in the main cabin was no comfort. Sam was scared on the last passage, but this was a different kind of fear. The thought of being lost in the middle of the ocean was truly terrifying. Sam thought of Tristan, probably lying safely in his bed in Victoria. If they ever made it back, Sam would probably be the only grey-haired student at Glenlyon!

Finally, he couldn't stay in bed any longer. He swung off the bunk and opened the door of his cabin just a crack.

" ... must be broken," he heard his mom's voice sounding a little frantic. "What are we going to do? It's been twelve hours since our last fix, and the machine isn't even giving any information."

"I know, Pamela," his dad's voice answered. He too sounded grim. "The problem is that we're heading for such a tiny little island. Even experienced sailors with the best navigation equipment could have trouble finding this place. It has no elevation and is less than a mile across. I really think we should return to Hawaii and get the Sat Nav fixed. Hawaii will be easy to find because of its altitude. And we're only two days away."

"Michael, you're not serious," his mom broke in quickly. "Surely we can find Fanning Island if we really try. Look, it's approximately 1,000 miles away. That means we have at least six days to study all the navigation books and improve our celestial navigation skills. Meanwhile, we can keep a careful compass heading and maintain accurate records of speed, distance, and time. Besides, we took that celestial navigation course last April, so we shouldn't have a problem with it."

Sam pressed his ear closer to the crack in the door. He could hear someone begin to pace back and forth in the main cabin.

Dad sounded angry. "Look, our lives are at stake here. That course was a simple eight-hour crash course on a topic that usually takes six months to learn. We're inexperienced at this, and I really think it's unwise to take chances. What happens if we get all that way and don't find Fanning? Then what do we do? The next island south of Fanning is another 1,300 miles away.

We'll be lost, and won't know which way to turn. We don't even have a radio to call for help, and our provisions and fresh water won't last forever.''

"We've gotten this far. Surely we can perfect our celestial navigation skills if we have to. This is what our trip is all about. We planned to take on the risks of the sea, we chose to go without a radio because we don't want to rely on help. We have to face the reality of it and learn to survive out here without all the electronic backup. I say we head for Fanning, but you're the skipper so you have to make the final decision.''

"Look, the weather is good now, but what happens if it gets cloudy and we can't see the sun, moon or stars to take a celestial sight? We could get blown right off our compass course in a storm. I don't think you understand how serious this could be. I wouldn't mind if we were by ourselves, but we have two young children on board that we have to worry about.''

"Michael, we'll look really silly crawling back into Hawaii just because our Sat Nav is on the fritz," Mom answered. "Let's stop arguing about this and start figuring out our position. Every good sailor has to know how to navigate by the sun, moon and stars, and it's time we learned.''

The pacing stopped. Dad's voice sounded weary. "Okay, Pamela. I just hope we're not doing this just to save a little pride. I'd rather turn back and look a little silly than risk all of our lives.''

"We're not risking our lives because you and I are about to spend whatever time it takes to master celestial. Now, here's a book for you to read, I'll read this one, and when we're through we'll compare notes. One more thing, though; let's not tell the kids. I don't want to scare them.''

Sam gently closed his door and crawled back into bed. Why, oh why, was he such a snoop?

July 4

Good afternoon Tristan! I've got my tie on. Welcome to my essay!

How I Learned Celestial Navigation
by Sam Bendall

Guess what we're learning about today? You guessed it — celestial navigation. Dad first explained to us that this is a very primitive but reliable form of navigation, using a sextant as the only piece of equipment.

Charlie and I were each given our own plastic sextant that has a whole bunch of knobs and mirrors. Then Dad showed us how to look through the eyepiece towards the sun (but you can use the moon or the stars as well) and measure the angle of its position in relation to the horizon. Then when the sight is set, we scream "now," and Dad records the exact time (within seconds!) from his special watch that has time zones from all over the world. It's really important to get the exact time, because four seconds off means one mile of error in *Kluane*'s position. That means if we're a minute off, we'll have a fifteen-mile error. Now I know why Dad was worried about missing Fanning Island.

The End

Well not really, Tristan. Just the end of my report. While we were learning celestial with Dad, you should have seen my mom. She drove me crazy, running in and out of the cabin all morning long, taking sights and doing calculations. Once you get the angle from the sextant, there are a lot of mathematical calculations to do, and I don't think she has figured it all out yet.

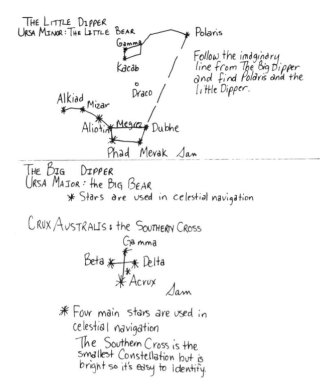

THE LITTLE DIPPER
URSA MINOR: THE LITTLE BEAR

Polaris

Follow the imaginary line from The Big Dipper and find Polaris and the little Dipper.

THE BIG DIPPER
URSA MAJOR: the BIG BEAR
✳ Stars are used in celestial navigation

CRUX AUSTRALIS: the SOUTHERN CROSS

✳ Four main stars are used in celestial navigation
The Southern Cross is the smallest Constellation but is bright so it's easy to identify.

The good news is that Kluane *is really sailing well today. Our hull speed sometimes reaches ten knots, and the seas are quite calm. We're really flying along. Dad says that if we continue at this speed, we'll cover more than 200 miles today. I love sailing when it's like this. Sometimes I take my Walkman onto the bow (with a safety line on of course) and listen to my favourite tunes while we skip across the waves. Fantastic.*

By the next day, Mom and Dad finally perfected their celestial calculations. They both did independent sights and calculations and landed on exactly the same spot. Since that spot corresponded with the one from their "dead reckoning" calculations on the chart, they could safely assume that they knew their position. The relief was overwhelming. Sam never let on that he knew how serious their situation had been, but it was hard to keep quiet about it, especially now that it was all right.

But their relief didn't last. The following day a huge blanket of clouds and bad weather descended on them. Now they had no way of finding their position, Sam realized. Mom and Dad spent every minute of the day with the sextant in one hand, searching for one peek of the sun through the skies, but nothing. There was still one more day before they were supposed to reach Fanning Island.

"Tomorrow I'll wake up and see clear skies," Sam muttered to himself as he rolled into his bunk that night.

But wishing for it didn't make it happen. The next morning was as dark as the day before. Mom and Dad barely spoke to each other as they searched the skies. It was so frustrating. All they needed was the clouds to clear a tiny bit — just for one minute.

By noon it was still overcast. The winds were picking up, and the sea was getting choppy. Even if the sky cleared, it would be difficult to take a celestial sight through the sextant when the seas were rough. It would be hard to get balanced and manage the sextant at the same time.

Thank heavens for Charlie, thought Sam. At least he was always cheerful and funny. It was easy to pretend that he didn't suspect anything was wrong, as long as Charlie was with him.

That night Sam found himself listening at the door of his room again. Sleep was the furthest thing from his mind. Mom and Dad were on deck, so Sam sat on the lowest rung of the steps as he strained to hear what they were saying.

"Michael, the sky looks as though it could be clearing further south of us. With any luck we can get a moon shot later on tonight. Can we both stay awake for all watches tonight just in case? We could just get lucky."

"I'm not so sure I'd be able to get much sleep anyway,"

Dad answered wearily. "I know we'll never be able to pick up any lights on Fanning Island because they probably don't even have electricity. Since we've had such strong winds over the past few days, we really have to keep a good watch out tonight, in case land is closer than we think. We better both be on the lookout for any signs of land — birds, dolphins, boats, anything."

July 7
Dear Tristan,

I didn't get a very good sleep last night because Mom and Dad were constantly scrambling around the deck above me. I'm sure I heard them say that they were able to get a moon shot, so let's hope we're all right. It's still really early in the morning, but I guess I'll get up now because Fanning Island should be getting close.

I just heard Dad and Mom setting the sails and wind vane again (that's the self-steering device) because they probably hove to during the night. I learned that when you want to stay in one spot on the ocean, you place the sails in such a way that they are working in opposite directions — called hove to. Dad probably placed Kluane hove to for the night because he didn't want to sail past Fanning Island and miss it in the darkness.

"All hands on deck!" called Dad suddenly. Sam dropped his pencil and flew out of his cabin.

"Crew, we have a very serious situation here, and I want your undivided attention." Sam had learned that when Dad spoke like that, you couldn't do anything else. "According to our calculations, Fanning Island is within six miles of us, directly ahead. We should have a sighting within the hour. Winds and currents could have taken us slightly off course so we must look in every direction for signs of land. Sam, you keep watch to port;

Pamela, to starboard; I'll look ahead, and Charlie can watch behind us.''

Each crew member sat motionless, waiting ...

Fifteen minutes had barely gone by when Dad jumped up and ran to the bow.

"Look! I see two tiny sticks standing on the horizon. They must be palm trees. Sam, bring me the binoculars, quickly." Sam got there instantly, as if he had wings. "Yup, we did it!" Dad shouted as he adjusted the lenses. "We found the needle in the haystack!"

With their safety lines attached, they all ran to the bow to see the wonderful sight for themselves. The skipper and his first mate hugged and kissed until Sam and Charlie became embarrassed. Then, Sam remembered that he wasn't supposed to know that they were in a potentially dangerous situation.

"What's all the excitement about?" he asked. "Why is everyone so surprised that we made it? The passage to Hawaii was three times as long, and we managed that one."

So they all sat down and listened, while their mother confessed the whole story.

As they approached Fanning Island, they had barely seen the outline of the land when the dolphins came to welcome *Kluane*. They did a fantastic show, with some of the dolphins jumping as high as six feet out of the water. Then from a little distance away, they heard screams coming from shore. As *Kluane* got closer, hoards of people began to line the entire shore, cheering the boat in. What a welcome! The customs officer later explained that as soon as one villager saw *Kluane* far in the distance, he ran through the village telling everyone, and they even let the school kids out early. The customs officer said they haven't seen white children before on the island (which Sam found hard to believe), but needless to say, *Kluane* and her crew were very special.

The excitement of approaching land was dampened quickly when the boat came close enough to Fanning to see three shipwrecks at the entrance to the lagoon. Those wrecks reminded them all that one mistake could cost them their lives. They had to proceed through the channel entrance at a snail's pace. No one was more relieved than Sam when the anchor was finally secured.

6. Living Off the Land

July 8

Dear Tristan,

Now I know what movie stars must feel like. Tony, the customs officer, invited us on a tour of the island today. You wouldn't believe the fuss they made over us. This island only gets three supply ships a year, and there are no planes or ferries either. Mom mailed some birthday cards today, which will probably take three months to arrive in Canada. (The birthdays are next week!)

The tour consisted of a walk to the tiny post office/police station (all in one room), school, and hospital. The hospital was so basic, we thought it was a vet's office at first. We learned that there are four hundred people living here, and their origin is KIRIBATI (pronounced KIRIBAS).

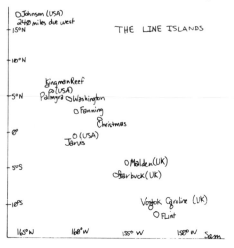

The strangest thing of all was that the villagers kept wanting to touch us. They followed us everywhere, just like the Pied Piper, and any time Charlie or I would stop for a second, they would touch our skin and hair. I haven't had so much attention in my whole life!

Here's another school report (Mom made me do it):

The Coconut Tree
by Sam Bendall

If the people of Fanning Island didn't have coconut trees, I don't think they could live. First, the tree and branches provide shade from the sun. From weaving the palms, they get mats and walls for their homes and thatch for the roofs. The trunk can be used for timber. The shells of the coconut are dried and used as containers for eating (bowls and cups), as well as charcoal for cooking. The coconut meat and milk provide nutritious food and drink, as well as coconut cream, which is a real delicacy. We've also noticed that the Islanders get their alcohol from hanging bottles of coconut milk in the trees and leaving it to ferment.

The only income these Fanning Islanders make is through the sale of "copra" (dried coconut meat) to foreign countries. Coconut oil from the pressed copra is used for making cosmetics, detergent, paint bases, and a great variety of skin oils. Finally, the husks of the coconuts (hairy looking) are braided to make rope and twine, flooring, matting, as well as cooking fuel.

When we told the local children that we didn't have coconuts in Canada, they looked pretty upset and wondered how we managed. I decided not to tell them about our huge shopping malls!

USES OF THE COCONUT PALM TREE

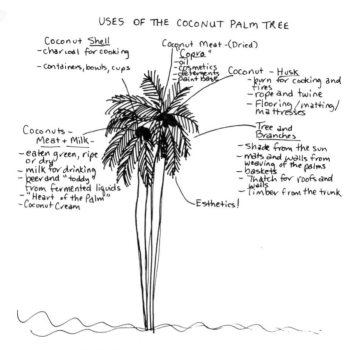

Coconut **Shell**
- charcoal for cooking
- containers, bowls, cups

Coconut Meat - (Dried)
"Copra"
- oil
- cosmetics
- detergents
- paint base

Coconut - **Husk**
- burn for cooking and fires
- rope and twine
- Flooring/matting/mattresses

Coconuts -
Meat + Milk -
- eaten green, ripe or dry
- milk for drinking
- beer and "toddy" from fermented liquids
- "Heart of the Palm"
- Coconut Cream

Tree and Branches
- Shade from the sun
- mats and walls from weaving of the palms
- baskets
- Thatch for roofs and walls
- Timber from the trunk

- Esthetics!

At the end of the tour, the village leader gave the family generous donations of bananas, papayas, breadfruit (which looked like a large green cantaloupe but tasted more like a potato), and coconuts. The leader promised them a tour of a bird sanctuary at the other end of the lagoon the next day. But the attention didn't stop there. The children, with gestures and broken English, asked Sam and Charlie to go swimming. After playing in the water for only a few minutes, the boys decided to return to *Kluane*. They could barely move, even in the water. At every turn, they were practically engulfed by the pressing children, who were fascinated by their pale complexions and fair hair. Sam decided it wasn't such a great thing to be a celebrity. Charlie, who had endured constant pats on the head since they had arrived in Fanning, gave his brother a look of desperation. Sam grabbed his brother's arm and began to work their way back to shore. Smiling and waving, the boys retreated, walking backwards almost the whole way to the protection of *Kluane*.

July 9

Dear Tristan,

I saw a shark today! We went to the bird sanctuary in a pickup truck owned by one of the churches (there are two trucks on the island, and just one road!). The driver of the truck only had one leg, so he used a stick as his right leg to press down the gas. At first we didn't notice that anything was wrong, except that he only had two speeds — fast and nothing. One minute we were stopped, and then suddenly we'd be going faster than the speed of light down a tiny dirt road. We had to hang on for our lives!

Anyway, Mom and Dad were busy admiring all the beautiful birds at one of the beaches, so Charlie and I decided to play in the sand. Without even thinking, I threw a rock into the water, and in seconds a shark appeared from nowhere. Boy, was he fast! He wasn't too big, but he sure looked fierce, with a black fin across his back and a long pointed snout.

Charlie said, "So much for swimming on this beach. I'm not going near that water!"

So Charlie and I began throwing more rocks and sticks into the water and played chicken with the sharks all afternoon. As long as we stood a few feet from the water's edge, we knew we were safe.

Scary, eh?

July 11

Dear Tristan,

We are now at Palmyra Island, about 200 miles northwest of Fanning Island. Dad decided to change locations because Fanning Islanders suffocated us too much. Charlie refused to even leave the boat after the second day, because they would *never leave him alone. We were also really bothered by all the flies on the island.*

And we all got these weird skin sores on Fanning Island. Dad doesn't know what it's from, but now we have skin infections all over our legs and feet. Dad has to put medicine on the sores every morning and evening, as well as after swimming in the salt water.

The only problem we had coming here was that there was no wind, so we had to motor the entire 200 miles. Normally that wouldn't be a problem, but Palmyra is completely undeveloped, so I know Dad is worried about a diesel shortage. Kluane's diesel tanks only hold 100 gallons, which isn't very much when you consider that we still have another 1,600 miles before the next diesel station in Samoa.

Palmyra has to be the most beautiful place in the world. The only inhabitants are two of the friendliest mongrel dogs, named Army and Palmyra, who swam out to meet us when we arrived. These dogs eat sharks! We actually saw Palmyra just swim out and take on a shark alongside Kluane. At first it was hard to tell what was happening — all we saw was the shark fin. Then, before we knew it, Palmyra was attacking the shark and swimming back to shore with the fish in his mouth. The people on the boat beside us said it happens all the time.

Four other yachts are anchored here beside us, and several of them have kids, so I know we'll have fun here. Mom and Dad are inflating the dinghy now so that we can go and look around the island.

First the family decided to explore the area by taking a walk all around the island. It was beautiful. Mom pointed out banana trees and breadfruit trees, with their huge green leaves. And of course there were palm trees — so many, they were impossible to count.

No one seemed to live there. Dad told them that Palmyra had at one time been an American army base. That explained a lot, thought Sam, as they spotted the neglected buildings and machinery which looked long abandoned. Running on ahead, Sam and Charlie found rusted out hulls of boats, old motors, and pipes, all overrun with spider webs and little hermit crabs.

The best discovery was a holding tank with what looked like an unlimited supply of fresh water. This meant *Kluane*'s tanks could be filled, and everyone could have a shower.

"Hey, Mom! There's a bathtub in the woods over here," cried Charlie, who had been doing some exploring on his own. Sure enough, when Charlie led the family down a jungle-like pathway, they found a bathtub lying in the bushes just waiting for someone to make use of it.

Mom clapped her hands. "All right, down to business. I've got myself a laundry tub!"

Back they trooped to *Kluane* to get their towels, shampoo and soap. Once they returned to the shower area, they all took turns standing under the cool freshwater tap. Mom had brought a bag of laundry for washing in the bathtub, but when she began her chores she thought of a new idea.

"Forget the laundry," she said. "I'm having a bath!"

All she had for bubbles was Joy dishwater detergent and laundry soap, but one could never be too fussy when there was nothing else. Before long she was soaking in the cool, fresh water and gazing into the banana trees above, with detergent bubbles frothing over the sides of the bathtub. There was no point in waiting around to help, Sam decided happily. She'd be there for at least an hour before getting down to the laundry.

Charlie and Sam continued on with their exploration of the

island. Charlie ran on ahead, hopping and cartwheeling in the sand, while Sam followed more slowly, and looked around. It was peaceful and still; completely different from Fanning. The shore was lined with trees and vegetation as thick as any jungle. Suddenly, under the branches of a huge tree that overhung the water, Sam walked straight into a heavy rope. Grabbing it, he looked up. The rope was looped at his end and securely tied to a main branch.

"Hey, Charlie," he called excitedly, "come here! See this rope in the tree?"

Charlie joined his brother and surveyed the rope swing doubtfully. "We prob'ly shouldn't play on it. Maybe we better get Dad."

Sam was disgusted. There were times Charlie could be a real wimp. "Look," he said emphatically, "all you have to do is climb onto the rope, hold on real tight, then swing down and drop into the water. You go first and I'll stand here in case you need help."

But Charlie wasn't buying that. "No way," he cried. "You go first, and I'll watch you!"

Sam had no choice but to give it a try. He climbed up the tree and cautiously took hold of the rope. Then, after taking a deep breath, he swung off the tree and landed with a big splash in the water below. This was great! He surfaced quickly and called for Charlie to try it.

Soon the boys were taking turns swinging off the rope. Before long they were attempting braver and braver ways of landing in the water — head first, cannonballs, twists, and even somersaults. The water was so warm, they could have played at this all day. Sam had a fleeting memory of the sharks they'd seen in the water from *Kluane*, but they were having too much fun to worry about it.

After at least an hour, Charlie hung onto the rope and looked around the island from his vantage point.

"Hey Sam," he said, "I see something through the trees. It looks like an airplane."

"No way, you're crazy," Sam answered. "Get off the swing if you're not going to jump."

Charlie hopped down and grabbed his older brother's arm. "Really. Come on, let's go check it out."

"Oh all right," Sam made his voice sound exasperated as he allowed himself be dragged away. He was getting tired of the swing anyway. The boys followed a narrow pathway through the forest.

"Oh yuck, spiderwebs," Charlie cried, wiping his arms and face. He pushed his brother forward. "Sam, you go first."

"Charlie, you really are a wimp sometimes," Sam sighed, but he took the lead, arms out to ward off the sticky webs. At last they came to a clearing. Charlie was right. Ahead of them stretched an old runway, and at one end sat a wrecked airplane. The plane must have crashed, because the entire front end was destroyed, but the cockpit was intact and definitely worth exploring.

Charlie and Sam climbed aboard the wing of the plane and peeked inside the cockpit. Charlie carefully pried open the door to the cabin with his eyes glued to the panel of buttons on the dashboard. He managed to squeeze his body into the pilot's seat.

"I want to be a pilot when I grow up, you know," said Charlie in a matter-of-fact tone.

Sam sat in the passenger seat while Charlie played with the controls, and then the boys took turns pushing all the buttons. The rest of the afternoon was glorious. Palmyra had the biggest and best toys they'd played with since leaving Victoria, Sam decided.

That night, all the sailors from the other yachts invited *Kluane*'s crew for dinner at the Palmyra Yacht Club. The "club" consisted of an old abandoned army building that visiting sailors had fixed up for socializing. The menu included fresh fish caught right in the lagoon, as well as lots of variations of breadfruit, coconut, and banana recipes.

The kids from the other yachts were all a little older than Sam and Charlie, but were more than friendly. No one seemed to care how old anyone else was. It was great to have company after such a long time at sea with no new faces.

"Have you ever caught a land crab?" asked Frank, one of the teenagers who had been there the longest.

"I don't even know what it is," admitted Sam.

Frank smiled knowingly. "If you want to make your mom and dad happy, I'll let you in on a secret. Land crabs are a real delicacy for adults, and I know a special spot where you can catch millions of them.

"You have to go in the dinghy right to the other side of the lagoon," he added, pointing out the general direction. "You'll know you're in the right spot because these land crabs are so thick, you won't even be able to land the dinghy without stepping on a few."

Sam and Charlie looked at each other uncertainly. "So . . . so how do we catch them?" Charlie asked.

"Easy," Frank replied. "Each person needs to get a stick that's forked at the end. You pair up in teams of two. Then, just hunt down a crab and have one person hold the crab down with the stick and the other one tear off the claw. Simple. Take a huge bucket with you, 'cause I guarantee you'll find more than you can handle."

It sounded pretty gross to Sam. He didn't care how happy it

made Mom and Dad, because there was no way he could handle something like that.

"One thing, though," Frank added. "Be sure you know the difference between a land crab and a coconut crab. The land crab looks just like a crab you'd find in the water, except it runs around on land, and it's smaller. You won't hurt it by taking a claw, because they can grow a new claw to replace the ones they lose. Coconut crabs are different. They're vicious and can really bite you if they attack. The coconut crab can't regenerate a new claw, so you'll be leaving it defenceless if you take one. In fact, they're becoming extinct now because so many people are harming them. You'll know the coconut crab when you see it because it's all hairy, much bigger then the land crab, and really looks fierce. Good luck."

The boys thanked Frank for the information. No way, Sam decided. He wouldn't even suggest it to Mom and Dad.

But the next day, after Sam and Charlie wolfed down the most delicious banana pancakes, Dad called a family meeting.

"Boys, it's time we all learned how to live off the land. If we want to stay in this place any longer, we are going to have to survive off the fish and fruits available here. Our provisions are getting pretty low, so we need to save what we have on *Kluane* for the passage to Samoa. From now on, anything we eat while we are here will come from the land and sea. What do you think we can find, Charlie?"

"Fish, breadfruit, coconuts, bananas. That's all I know," Charlie replied quickly. He looked innocently at his older brother.

"And Sam?" Dad asked. "Can you think of anything else?"

Sam couldn't think of anything except Frank's horrible

secret. "Well, I do have an idea," he said reluctantly. "We'll need to use the dinghy for this, and we'll need a bucket. Follow me."

Mom and Dad were so amazed that Sam was taking charge, they didn't even question where they were going. They followed Sam into the dinghy, *Kluane II Too.*

The crab area was just as Frank had described it. Land crabs were everywhere. The sand was barely visible.

"Wow, dinner!" shouted Mom.

Sam gulped. He couldn't chicken out. He gave them all a lesson on how to catch the crabs, just as Frank had described. The family formed two teams: Mom and Sam, and Dad and Charlie. It took a while to get started, since everyone was a little reluctant to try. But before long, they found themselves scrambling over the sand, catching as many crab claws as they could. The bucket was overflowing in no time! Frank was right, Sam thought later. Mom and Dad were practically drooling over the claws. There would be quite a feast to take to the Palmyra Yacht Club tonight. And Frank wouldn't think Sam was such a wimp after all.

July 15
Dear Tristan,

I wish we didn't have to leave tomorrow, but Dad is really getting worried about the lack of diesel. We have managed to do really well getting food every day, though. It usually takes all morning to get enough fish and fruit for the day, and then our afternoons are spent playing. We had delicious banana pancakes every morning and fish for lunch and dinner, along with our favourite — breadfruit french fries.

Dad and I will spend the rest of today filling our water tanks with fresh water, while Mom will get all the laundry finished. She pressure-canned lots of fish for the next passage to Samoa. I know that once she has her work all done, she'll spend the rest of the day in the bathtub. Charlie is going to really miss Army and Palmyra when we leave, so he'll probably play with them all day.

Tonight we'll have our final feast with these sailors because they are all heading north to Hawaii, and we're heading south. I know I'll miss them, especially Frank. It's been so nice to have someone close to my age to talk to, besides you.

7.   Crossing the Equator

Dad was determined to leave Palmyra at daybreak the following day, so everyone said their farewells at the social hour the night before. But Charlie never got a chance to say good-bye to his friends Army and Palmyra. Charlie was still asleep when *Kluane* left the lagoon that morning.

Knowing that the best fishing was in the channel at the entrance to the lagoon, Sam was keen to put out a fishing line. The line was barely in the water before a red grouper had taken its lure.

"Better put it back, Sammy," Dad shouted from the helm. "Some kinds of red fish can be poisonous. We can't take a chance." Sam hated to put a catch back. But as he unhooked the little fish and watched it slide back into the sea, he suddenly found himself almost nose-to-nose with a tuna. Soon a huge school of them started jumping all around *Kluane*.

"Wow, Mom, Dad — tuna!"

The excitement aboard *Kluane* was beyond control. Dad shouted orders from the helm. His hands weren't free, and he had no choice but to guide the boat safely through the narrow channel, treacherously lined with huge coral heads that could tear the hull apart in seconds. Sam and Charlie prepared the fishing lines for tuna, and Mom ran between Dad and the boys, taking orders from the frantic skipper. Everyone was madly scrambling around *Kluane*'s deck.

Then, "Kaboom!"

A huge explosion came from the engine compartment. Everything went dead. The engine conked out, the electronics stopped beeping, Mom, Dad, and even Sam and Charlie stood frozen in position with their mouths open.

Suddenly Dad sprang into action. He ran inside the cabin to check the bilges in case water was coming in through a hole in the hull. Mom grabbed the helm and adjusted the sails to steer *Kluane* as far away from the reef as possible. Heading back to Palmyra was out of the question because it would be too dangerous to go through the narrow channel without an engine. It was even impossible to radio for help from their friends because none of the electronics — including the radio — worked.

The boys hung over either side, watching for the reef. Sam's heart was beating so fast, he could feel it throb in his ears. Sam looked in every direction for signs of tuna, but there were none. Even the fish must have been scared away by the explosion. He chewed his lip anxiously. The first hour of a 1,600 mile passage and they were already in trouble. Not a good sign. Now, *Kluane* would only have the use of her sails and a sextant until the problem was fixed.

"It doesn't look too serious," called Dad from the engine room. "The engine's fan belt broke, which made the engine overheat. That explosion was just the self-releasing fire extinguisher doing its job so the engine wouldn't overheat completely. Stay on this course, Pamela, while I fix the fan belt."

Mom shouted back, "How long?"

"It could be a while. There's foam from the fire extinguisher all over the engine compartment."

Sam went below to give his dad a hand repairing the engine. The heat was unbearable. As he wiped the perspiration from his forehead, Sam remembered their lesson on the equator. Yes, the heat was definitely more intense the closer they got. Fresh water was too precious to be used for cooling off, so they could only resort to salt water. But even that was warm.

By midday, the engine was fixed, and *Kluane* was back on course. Sam couldn't believe how one tiny fan belt could cause so many problems — including the loss of some prized tuna!

July 19
Dear Tristan,

It's getting pretty boring out here. As we get closer to the equator, the winds are becoming milder. In fact, we can barely get enough wind into our sails to keep them filled in order to move forward. I may have to begin my correspondence schooling just for something to do. Now, that's desperate!

"This condition is called 'the doldrums,'" Dad explained later. "It's very common to have less wind around the equator, but let's hope it doesn't last too long."

"Why can't we just turn on the engine, Dad?" Charlie asked.

"Two reasons," he answered. "First, we happen to be on a sailboat. If we wanted to motor across the ocean we would have bought a motor boat. Second, we have a very limited supply of diesel now. We need to have enough on reserve in order to charge our batteries every second day that we are at sea, and still leave some for motoring into port when we arrive in Western Samoa."

"At least we don't have to worry about getting seasick," Sam offered.

Mom laughed. "Thank goodness for that. We'll just have to be patient; we could be here for some time. We have 300 miles before we reach the equator, so try to get used to this. Perhaps this is a good time to begin your school studies."

Sam groaned. Just what he'd been afraid of. Time to put on

the old school tie again. Oh well, at least they could look forward
to the equator party. Crossing the equator was always a big event
for every sailor, so they knew Mom would do something special.

July 20
Dear Tristan,

*Guess what? Mom just calculated our distance for
yesterday. We covered 30 miles . . .BACKWARDS! We are now
going so slowly we are actually going backwards. I accidentally
threw a paper jet overboard last night, and it was still floating
beside us when I got up this morning! I guess I'll give in and start
my correspondence work today. It's going to be strange having
my mother as a teacher.*

"Ring, ring!" cried Mom, as she stuck her head in Sam's
cabin. Sam looked up from his diary and grimaced. School was
in.

Mom grinned. "Well Sammy, we have a lot of work to do if
you want to have grade five completed by next September, so
let's begin by making a timetable to make sure you don't get
behind." She turned and led Sam into the main cabin. Sam
followed behind, tongue stuck out, while he held the ends of his
tie up in the air like a hangman's rope.

Mom ignored him. "Let's see, there are thirty lessons, so if
we complete one lesson every two weeks, we should have enough
time for all the work and still have a summer holiday before
grade six."

"Does that mean I have to go to school on weekends?"
asked Sam, piteously.

"You can go to school whenever you want, because it's right
here in the cabin. But just remember, the sooner you get it done,

the sooner you'll have holidays. This work all has to be completed — it won't disappear, so it's up to you to motivate yourself." Mom continued to look through the reams of papers she carried in her arms. "I see that your teacher's name is Mr. Maddison and he lives near Victoria. Since he's the correspondence teacher for the B.C. School Board, he must have some interesting kids in his class who are doing all sorts of things like we are. I wish we had a picture of Mr. Maddison so we know what he looks like, don't you?"

No, Sam thought, not really. Unless I had a dart board to pin it onto. "Do I have any tests to write?" he asked aloud.

Mom shook her head, as she poured over the material. "It looks like the whole year is just one big test. You'll be marked on everything you do, and that will account for your final mark. Your only subjects are mathematics, English, science, and social studies, so you should be able to handle it well. Now, let's get started so that you can mail in your first lesson from Western Samoa."

Sam made a face. She was already sounding just like a teacher.

From that day on, a routine was established. Mom would spend time at the beginning of school each day, reviewing the material that Sam was required to learn in each subject. Once Sam understood the job for the day, he would work on his own, calling for help if he was stuck.

Sometimes it was hard to concentrate and stay motivated. At times, Sam wanted to do anything else — even clean his cabin. Here he was, stuck in the middle of nowhere, and he was in school! Everyone ignored him — even Charlie, who had been warned to leave Sam alone when he was working. There was no one to complain to, no one to listen to his sighs and groans. And, worst of all, he had to do it right. Mom had warned him that any incorrect work mailed from Samoa would just be returned to their next destination. And the last thing he wanted was the opportunity to do it over again!

July 21

Dear Tristan,

We still seem to be going nowhere, but every once in a while there is a small puff of wind that takes us a little farther. Mom and Dad are thinking of all sorts of things to keep us entertained while we're stuck out here. Today, Charlie and I learned some really neat sailor's knots — the bowline, clove hitch, reef knot, and stopper knot. Dad is going to test us on these knots tomorrow, so I've been practising all afternoon. It's amazing how many knots you can do on a sailboat — we have a whole book of them on board. After Dad's lesson on knots, Charlie and I began looking through the knot book for other kinds of knots to try. Soon we had knots tied everywhere on Kluane. Some kinds are used for tying things together, others are used for support, and there is even one that is so strong you can hang from it — Charlie loved that one.

We have also started to play a game that is really fun. The clouds in this area at sunset always form really interesting shapes and lie just along the horizon. Every evening, we all gather in the cockpit to watch the sun go down, and while we are sitting there, we all make a story from an imaginary shape somewhere in the clouds. Charlie always has the funniest stories because his imagination is incredible.

I can't believe how beautiful the sunsets are out here. We always watch as the sun hits the horizon, because sometimes on a really clear night, you're supposed to be able to see a bright green flash appear just as the sun disappears behind the horizon. We always watch for the flash but haven't seen one yet. Oh well, it gives us something to do!

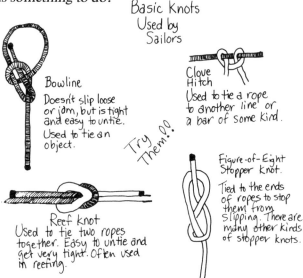

Basic Knots
Used by
Sailors

Bowline
Doesn't slip loose or jam, but is tight and easy to untie. Used to tie an object.

Clove Hitch
Used to tie a rope to another line or a bar of some kind.

Try Them!

Reef Knot
Used to tie two ropes together. Easy to untie and get very tight. Often used in reefing.

Figure-of-Eight Stopper Knot.
Tied to the ends of ropes to stop them from slipping. There are many other kinds of stopper knots.

Gradually, *Kluane* limped towards the equator. The heat became so intense, that wearing any clothing besides their bathing suits was unbearable. Finally, one morning Mom couldn't stand it any longer.

"That's it. I'm going for a swim," she announced.

"Mom, you can't," Sam was incredulous. "There's 12,000 feet of water below us. You don't know what's down there."

"Yeah," Charlie piped up, "what about sharks 'n stuff!"

But Mom was already securing a rope around her waist. "I'm too hot to care," she answered. "I'm going in anyway. If I start to yell, just pull me in." With that remark, she slipped off the transom and floated happily behind the boat.

Sam shuddered. There was no way he'd jump in, with more than a mile of ocean (and anything that might be in it) below him. Charlie had no interest in it either. But once Mom was back on board, Dad could not resist the temptation. He plunged in with a huge splash, then lay on the surface of the water, his legs and arms straight out like a starfish.

"This is heaven," he cried, while Sam and Charlie shook their heads. Mom and Dad were really crazy.

July 22
Dear Tristan,

Today we finally crossed the equator! Charlie thought it was kind of dumb to make a fuss, since the water didn't look any different, but when Mom reminded him of the party, he got pretty excited.

Mom said we had to dress up in costumes, so Charlie and I wrapped ourselves up in a sheet and pretended to be a bed. Dad made a mask out of foil and called himself "the gremlin of the deep," and Mom rolled herself up in toilet paper and came as a roll of — guess what — toilet paper! Oh well, it's hard to find costumes out here. We had streamers and balloons, and Charlie and I got some books and art supplies as gifts.

Now that we've made it to the equator, it looks like we may be here for a little while. The breeze has disappeared again (if you can even call it a breeze).

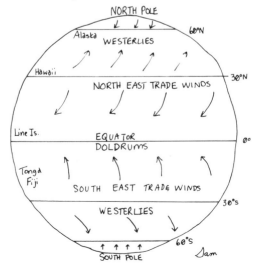

Four more days passed without wind or any sign of life beyond *Kluane*. There were no fish. Even the albatrosses deserted them, because without wind, the big birds couldn't fly. Charlie, unlike his usual manner, hardly spoke at all. Maybe that was because the food was so boring, Sam thought. They had run out of fresh fruits and vegetables long ago and were now relying on canned foods for most of their meals.

Kluane still had over a thousand miles to cover before they would reach Samoa. Sam began to wonder if they would ever make it. They were more than two weeks over their estimated date of arrival. If family and friends didn't hear from them soon, they might think *Kluane* was lost at sea. Without either a single-side band or ham radio, they had no way of communicating to anyone that they were safe.

The diesel supply was becoming so low, that soon there wouldn't be enough to charge the batteries to run their power on board. No one said anything about it, but the situation looked pretty grim.

Then one morning, when Mom was on watch, Sam was jolted out of bed.

"A ship!" she called. "I can't believe it . . . a ship!"

Everyone stumbled to the cockpit. It was like magic. A ship was visible, far in the distance, but definitely a ship.

Dad had his binoculars trained on the sight. "It looks like a tanker," he said. "She appears to be moving away from us."

"I'm going to try to call her up on the marine radio," Mom said, disappearing below.

"Can they give us a ride?" Charlie asked.

Dad laughed. "No. But they can contact some people for us, just to let them know that we're all right. And maybe," he added, "they can give us some diesel."

Mom called from the main cabin. "Michael, they're not responding to my call."

"Dad," Sam pleaded, "can't we light a flare?"

Flares were only to be used in cases of extreme emergency, Sam and Charlie had been told. There were two colours, however. The red flare was the real distress flare, indicating that the ship was in danger. The white flare was set off just to attract attention.

Dad hesitated for only a second. "All right," he said. "We'll try a white flare. You boys get some flags."

While Sam and Charlie waved flags and shouted, Dad shot a flare, which popped into the sky with a satisfying burst of light. Nothing happened at first, but then after a few moments, the ship altered course and headed straight for *Kluane*.

"Sam," Dad said quickly, "go below and get Mom to help you put together the biggest sign you can. Print 'diesel please' on it."

Sam flew along the deck to do as he was told. Soon he and Mom were back on deck with the sign in their hands between them. Finally the tanker was within a quarter of a mile of *Kluane*. Sam and Charlie hoisted the sign high above their heads. Sam couldn't see anyone on deck; the ship was big, black and looked deserted, but someone had to be on board. Sam resumed his waving.

"Do you think they'll have ice cream?" Charlie asked. "Maybe we should ask for ice cream."

Mom ignored Charlie. "I can't understand why they didn't answer my call. We have to relay a safety message too."

"We can do that when they give us the fuel," Dad answered.

Then, in spite of the sign high above Sam and Charlie's

heads, the ship changed course.

Sam was incredulous. "They saw us. Why are they turning around?" It was beyond belief, but it was happening. Slowly at first, but now picking up speed, the tanker turned and headed away from *Kluane*.

"Hey, come back!" Charlie shouted.

Sam and Charlie slowly lowered the sign. "Michael, they must have seen us," Mom cried out in disbelief. "How could they just leave without even finding out our name?"

Sam was overwhelmed by a sense of panic. "Dad, please can't we start up the engine and follow it?"

Dad shook his head slowly. "We can't risk it, Sam. We'd never catch her, and we'd use up the last of our fuel."

The family silently watched as the tanker's black silhouette gently faded into the horizon. The ship had come and gone like a dream. And now they were alone again. For how long, no one dared think.

"So," Mom said finally, "we'll just have to stop worrying about everyone at home, that's all. I'm going to make some bread." And with that, she turned and went below.

When Mother Nature decides to show her stuff, she does it in style. One morning Dad pointed out a line of dark clouds on the horizon. The knot meter began to creep up from zero to one, then to four within the hour. Soon they were moving so quickly that Mom and Sam ran below to put their gear away.

"Hey Pam," Dad shouted from the helm, "at the rate we're going, I'm going to need you to reef the sails."

At last they were moving. After two weeks of dead calm, *Kluane* was now averaging 170 miles a day. Strong, steady winds kept them hopping for the rest of the journey. Before they knew it, Samoa was on the horizon.

"All right!" Charlie shouted. "Ice cream!"

8.   A New Lesson

As *Kluane* pulled into the customs dock in Apia Harbour, Sam and Charlie stood on the foredeck and hung over the railing, entranced by the activity in the harbour. This was obviously a foreign country, Sam thought. A lot more foreign than Hawaii had been.

Charlie nudged his brother. "Hey Sam, don't look now but that man is wearing a skirt! Gosh, all the men are wearing skirts!"

"Don't point," Sam hissed, as he grabbed Charlie's arm. "Boy, I hope they don't expect us to wear one. Mom says that she has to wear long skirts all the time here because women can't even wear shorts."

The town of Apia was tiny and seemed quite poor, but it was clean and looked well tended. Both Sam and Charlie were relieved when the customs officer told them that all the paperwork had been accepted, and how they could explore this new country.

The first stop was the telephone office, where Mom wanted to place a call to Canada to tell friends and family they were safe. But when the family trooped into the telephone office building, a huge line-up greeted them. People were sitting all over the office floor, on benches, and even outside on the sidewalk waiting for their turn. The office worker gave Mom a telephone appointment for 11:00 a.m.

"We have one hour before I have to return to this office,"

said Mom. "Let's go and explore the town. Maybe we can begin our search for the best ice cream shop."

The boys needed no encouragement. Charlie, of course, was first to find a little store with a counter and stools they could climb up on. Once the boys had devoured their first ice cream cones in ages, it was obvious they had loads of room in their tummies for more. Next came a milkshake each, followed by a large glass of cold milk. Finally, their cravings were satisfied and they were able to think of other things.

Soon it was time to return to the phone company, so Sam went with Mom, while Charlie and Dad set off to find a grocery store.

At the office, Sam and Mom sat quietly, waiting for their name to be called. Sam's white skin and blond hair attracted many stares from around the room, followed by huge friendly smiles.

After what seemed like hours, Mom turned to the Samoan man sitting beside her. "What time is your telephone appointment?" she asked.

"Four thirty," he replied.

"Do you mean that you're going to wait here all day?" Mom sounded amazed.

"No, just until four thirty," he answered, with a curious expression, as if to say, "What's wrong with that?"

Sam and Mom looked at each other. They'd never see this kind of patience in North America. But if a Samoan was content to spend the next six hours or so in the office, then they could too, Sam thought.

"Sam," Mom said slowly, "I think we'd better just sit back and relax like the rest of our friends here. We could be waiting a very long time."

August 3

Dear Tristan,

Boy, is it ever different in this place. I'm really starting to appreciate how wonderful Canada is. Today we had to spend over two hours waiting to make a phone call. They only have one telephone office here, with six phones. All the phones are in one room, so once we did finally get our turn, we could hardly hear the conversation because everyone else in the room was making so much noise. Mom called Canada, and it's lucky that she did, because our friends were just beginning to organize a search for us.

We went to the market to get food, but it's nothing like shopping in Canada. This market is open all day and night so the Samoan people who have tables at the market actually sleep right at their stalls the whole night long. Huge stands of every fruit and vegetable grown in the country are sold here — papayas, coconuts, bananas, breadfruit and many kinds of fish are just some examples of what we bought. Even the fenceposts grow here!

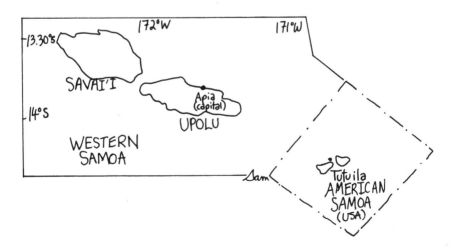

The next day, the family explored a popular snorkelling area and spent the afternoon swimming and relaxing. Sailors from several nearby yachts came by to introduce themselves, and everyone agreed to meet for supper at the local Chinese restaurant later.

As always, *Kluane II Too* was secured properly on the beach. Off they went to the restaurant, completely unaware of the events that lay ahead.

The family met many new friends at dinner, and enjoyed the wonderful meal. But when they returned to the spot where *Kluane II Too* had been left, she was nowhere in sight. At first, Sam couldn't believe it. He had just been named skipper of the little dinghy and was responsible for her security. He was certain the boat was secured properly. There was no way *Kluane II Too* could just drift away.

Then Sam's disbelief turned to anger. Anger at himself for not locking the dinghy, and anger towards the thieves, whoever they were. It was getting very late, and there was no way of returning to *Kluane* without a dinghy. They had to find it right away.

Sam and his dad searched the entire beach and found no trace of the dinghy or clues to its whereabouts. They finally concluded that she had been stolen, and Dad left them to find the police station.

"I don't believe this," said Sam, as the three of them crouched on the beach. "I should have secured the chain around a tree or something and locked it. Without the dinghy, we are really stranded, aren't we? We'll never find another one in Samoa."

"Sammy, don't worry," Mom answered, mussing his hair. "Things will work out." Mom was becoming a little too relaxed, Sam thought in exasperation. This place was really starting to affect her.

Soon a Samoan policeman arrived on the scene in a four-wheel drive vehicle, with Dad next to him in the front seat.

"Pamela, kids, this is Musolani," Dad said as they climbed out of the jeep.

Sam had already seen that Samoans were pretty large people, but he had never seen anyone as big as Musolani. This man was huge in every way — big hands, big feet, big stomach and a big smile to match. If anyone was going to find *Kluane II Too*, Sam thought, it would be Musolani.

After taking down all the relevant facts about *Kluane II Too*'s disappearance, Musolani and his Samoan helpers began their search of the entire beach area. The next two hours seemed like the longest Sam had ever lived through, and when Musolani returned in his four-wheel drive, he had nothing to report. By midnight, there was still no trace of the dinghy, so Musolani could only suggest that the family return to *Kluane* by police dinghy, and the search would resume the following day.

"I'll bet we never find *Kluane II Too*," grumbled Sam, while he sadly joined his family in the replacement dinghy and prepared himself for the ride out to *Kluane*.

"Listen!" he suddenly cried, standing up in the dinghy and pointing to the shore. "I hear sirens."

He was right. Only seconds later, a great stream of flashing lights from two assistant police vans appeared. To everyone's delight, an officer announced the dinghy had been found.

The police told them that two young Samoan boys, aged ten and eleven, decided to borrow *Kluane II Too* to go fishing. Sam could see the two boys sitting quietly in the back seat of the van, their eyes wide as they stared through the glass window. Sam could see that the boys were very frightened. At the same time, a policeman arrived by water in *Kluane II Too* and properly secured the dinghy on the beach.

Musolani turned to the family with an expression of deep

concern on his face. "I am very sorry for the inconvenience these two young Samoan boys have caused you. Before we ask the boys to apologize for their crime, I would like to explain something to you which may help you understand the situation better. In Samoa we have very special customs. Anything a Samoan owns is considered to belong to the entire village or community. We don't own many material things like western society people, and those things that we do own are shared with all our people.

"These boys don't believe they did anything wrong. They wanted to go fishing to catch food for their family, and this dinghy was available on the beach. They had every intention of returning the dinghy once they had finished fishing. We are facing a problem here of two types of cultures that don't completely understand each other. We do have to teach our young Samoans that white cultures consider it a crime to take things they don't own. Samoans are trying very hard to change, but such things always takes time."

Suddenly Sam began to feel sorry for the two young boys. It was a relief to get the dinghy back, of course. But something in him wished that they had never called the police in the first place. If they had waited long enough, the dinghy would have reappeared. It had been quite a learning experience for everyone. From now on he would always lock the dinghy, and the young Samoan boys would have to be more careful as well.

The two boys quietly whispered their apologies and were sent back to the police van which would take them to the police station.

"I wonder what kind of penalty those boys will get?" asked Sam as they rowed *Kluane II Too* quietly through the anchorage back to the boat.

"I was wondering the same thing," said Mom. "Let's walk

to the police station tomorrow morning and ask Musolani. Besides, he was so kind to us, I think it would be nice to ask him for dinner aboard *Kluane* one night.''

Early the very next day, Sam and his Mom set off for the police station. Musolani was happy to accept the invitation for dinner the following Monday night and told them how Samoan children were punished.

''We usually let the chief from their village handle discipline,'' he said. ''In Samoa, the chiefs have the highest power. Usually, a chief will ask the whole family to pay a fine or do work in the village. Often the parents have to pay the fines for their children's mistakes.''

If only he had been more careful to lock the dinghy properly, this would never have happened, Sam thought. If only they had understood more about the Samoans in the first place. Now maybe two whole families were being punished for one tiny misunderstanding. More than ever, he wished they had done nothing about it.

Early Monday morning, Sam heard his mother banging around in the galley. ''I have a lot of cooking to do if I'm going to fill Musolani's stomach,'' she exclaimed.

''But Mom,'' Sam cried, as he peered over her shoulder, ''that's enough spaghetti to feed a whole army. It looks like our entire six months' supply of provisions for one meal. Musolani couldn't eat that much, could he?''

''I don't know, I've never cooked for anyone even half his size,'' she answered, as she stirred the sauce. Then a thought hit her. She turned to Sam. ''I wonder how he'll fit into the dinghy. You'd better go by yourself to pick him up from shore. I'll bet his weight alone exceeds the maximum for that dinghy.''

But Musolani handled himself like a pro in the dinghy, and he and Sam arrived at *Kluane* just in time for evening cocktails.

"I'm very sorry that I am late," he remarked. "Mondays are always very busy for Samoan police. We have a custom in Samoa where all prisoners are allowed to visit their homes in their villages on weekends. So on Mondays, the police must always round up the prisoners and make sure they are back in jail. Today I spent more than twelve hours chasing prisoners through a pineapple plantation, so I'm pretty tired."

Charlie's eyes lit up as he listened to Musolani speak. No doubt the thought of running through pineapple plantations was appealing to Charlie, Sam thought. Now he'd be saying that he would like to be a policeman when he grows up.

As the evening progressed, Sam, Charlie, and their parents listened intently to Musolani's stories of village life. He emphasized how important cooperation was to the village, where the chief and elders were held in the utmost respect and younger family members looked after their elders.

"The family home is called a 'bure,' and often it holds as many as ten people living under one roof," Musolani explained. "It's common to have grandparents, parents and grandchildren all living in one home, and when someone dies, their grave lies right on the same property to keep the family together forever."

Musolani grinned widely and looked down at Sam and Charlie. "We have one Samoan tradition that you boys should like: the tattoo. It is mandatory for every chief to be tattooed, male or female, or they cannot attend chiefs' meetings. A tattoo is made by injecting ink with needles into deep layers of skin. This is permanent and very painful. Intricate designs are created which are usually symbolic to the person's heritage. Those who are brave enough to withstand the pain of many tattoos are highly respected within each village. Men traditionally tattoo their buttocks, waist, thighs, and face, while the women tattoo their groin, hips and thighs." Sam shuddered as he tried to imagine sitting still while needles were being stuck into him. No, he thought, that's one tradition I'm glad we don't have in Canada.

Sam was amazed by the amount of food his mother served Musolani. She just kept heaping the spaghetti onto his plate, and he devoured each serving in no time. Dad had told them before that larger people are highly respected in Samoa because it is a sign of having enough wealth to afford lots of food. Sam was even more surprised when he saw how much food Mom was eating. It seemed that for once she didn't have to worry about her waistline, knowing that larger people are more attractive in Samoa.

August 15
Dear Tristan,

I can't believe that we have already been here for two weeks. It's almost time to head for Tonga. The Samoan people have been incredibly friendly to us — especially Musolani, who visits us almost every day. Sometimes I wonder if we were lucky to lose Kluane II Too *that night, because we wouldn't have met Musolani or the other police officers otherwise.*

Also, I can't believe how much food we have eaten lately. Samoan food is so delicious. In a real Samoan feast we get to sit on the floor and eat with our fingers because they usually don't have utensils or much furniture. Most of the food is cooked in coconut cream, which makes it delicious.

Dad says I have to help him with chores tomorrow, since we are leaving any day now. It's not going to be much fun hauling 120 gallons of water in jerry cans and tons of diesel to Kluane *in this heat. There's a lot more work involved in being a sailor than I thought.*

No doubt about it, being a sailor was a lot of work, thought Sam as he struggled with a full can of water along the road. It took a lot of cans to fill *Kluane*'s tanks — enough it seemed to keep them in water for the rest of their lives. He had lost track of the number of times he had staggered back to the boat with a full tank. Five, maybe six? He stopped, put down his load, and wiped the sweat out of his eyes. Water was a lot heavier than he imagined.

Finally, after Sam had emptied the last jerry can of water into the tank, a man in an inspector's uniform came alongside in his dinghy.

"Good afternoon," he said politely, nodding to Dad. "I'm the Apia City Health Inspector. One of our officers advised me that you have been using the water from the dockside taps to fill your boat tanks. Is that correct?"

"Yes we have," Dad answered. "I hope there is no problem."

"In fact, I regret that there is a problem, sir, because our department has just completed a comprehensive study on the town's water and discovered that it is unfit for human consumption. I'm afraid to say that we recommend you do not drink that water."

"I don't believe it," Dad exploded. "We just hauled 120 gallons of that water by jerry can. We are about to leave for an ocean passage and need water in our tanks. My son and I are exhausted, and now you say we can't use the water? Please tell me where I can find suitable water in this town."

"I'm sorry sir, but I'm afraid all the water has been contaminated. We hope to solve the situation soon. I can only suggest that you put some kind of disinfectant into the water to kill any bacteria. It might not taste as good, but it will be safe."

The inspector zoomed away as quickly as he had arrived,

leaving a bewildered and exhausted crew. They were planning to leave Samoa early the following morning and had already officially cleared out of the country. They would have to find a solution quickly, because the Samoan government only allowed a boat to remain in the country twenty-four hours from the checkout time.

"It's ridiculous to wait here for the inspectors to give clearance on the water. That could take forever," Dad said finally. "We'll have to use the water in our tanks for cleaning and boil what we need for drinking. I guess we'll have to resort to buying soft drinks and pre-mixed juices for this passage. Kids, for the first and last times in your lives, we are going to insist that you drink lots of soft drinks, because that is our only choice for now."

"Awww, do we have to?" asked Sam sarcastically, while Charlie jumped for joy.

"Yup, it's a real shame. I can see you are both devastated. The heat is so intense here we must make sure we have an abundance of liquids aboard. This next passage should only take three days so I'm not too concerned. Here's the last of my Samoan money. Use this fifty dollars to buy whatever kinds of soft drinks you like. I would prefer a huge supply of juice, but the pre-watered juices are too expensive here. We have no choice but to buy all that unhealthy pop. Go for it boys."

Sam and Charlie didn't waste a second. They were in the dinghy and off to the store in no time, before their father got another, less appealing idea. They returned with four different selections of soft drinks, and two of the largest smiles on the island.

August 19
Dear Tristan,

Today, the most beautiful boat that I've ever seen arrived in our anchorage. It caught my eye when it was a long way from the harbour, and from that moment I could not think of anything else. Her name is Venture, and she is a Swan 46. Dad says that Swans are the Cadillac of boats, and I agree.

Once her anchor was secured, I had to go and see the boat close up, so I paddled over in Kluane II Too. The owners were cleaning the hull, and they stopped as soon as I came close. Their names are Dick and Nancy, and they are as wonderful as their boat. Dick asked me to invite the whole family for a visit. Of course, I couldn't wait to get Mom and Dad — I've never paddled so fast in my life.

Tristan, this boat has everything. There's not a thing missing. All the winches are motorized, everything is automatic, and it even has a freezer and microwave. I'm so glad we got to stay an extra day, because otherwise I would never have seen Venture. I think Mom and Dad get along really well with Dick and Nancy, so maybe we'll see them again in Tonga. I know they are headed that way as well.

We said good-bye to Musolani today. He was such a nice man. The only thing I don't like about this sailing life is having to say good-bye to all the great people we meet.

9. The Worst Storm

The sun had just peeked above the horizon when *Kluane's* anchor was lifted from the bottom of Apia Harbour. Preparing for any ocean passage always demanded critical thought and planning. The crew had to make sure the boat was completely safe and ready for whatever unexpected events that might occur during the passage. Once they were out of sight of land, the crew must survive without any assistance.

Dad led *Kluane* safely out of Apia Harbour, but not before they made one complete circle around *Venture* for one last look. Sam could not take his eyes off the sailboat. She was a masterpiece. One day, he thought, I want to own a boat just like her. From that time on, whenever Sam had a spare moment, he would take out his art supplies and draw *Venture* with all her beautiful lines and features.

Kluane was barely out of sight of land when the ocean swells became noticeably higher. Soon the waves climbed to heights no one had ever seen before. Reading and drawing became a chore. Only Charlie seemed thrilled to have such a violent ride; it was time to start tumbling across the cabin floor again.

"We may be in for a rough three days," Dad announced. "The wind is beginning to change direction. Unfortunately, we'll be heading straight into the wind, which means that we will have to tack the entire way. This will be a bumpy ride."

"Pamela," he continued tersely, "you'd better make sure that everything in the cabin is secured tightly."

August 20
Dear Tristan,

This trip to Tonga is not going to be fun. I can hardly even write, and the waves are getting higher by the minute. They are so high, it's like we are climbing a huge mountain every ten seconds. The worst part is that Kluane is really bashing around out here. Dad says that it's because we are heading directly into the wind. Since sailboats need wind in their sails to move forward (they can't sail directly into the wind), we have to tack, which makes our trip take even longer. Tacking means that we head slightly off course so that the wind is coming at an angle and filling our sails. So, when we've sailed a certain distance in one direction, we tack and steer the same angle from the wind in the other direction. I don't have to tell you that this means we cover a lot more distance and it will take us far longer than we planned to get to Tonga. At least we all seem to be over our seasickness.

When nightfall approached, the seas took on a frightful look, with swells mounting as high as forty feet. Sam could hear his parents working continuously in the cockpit as he lay in his bunk attempting to sleep.

"We'll have to take turns hand steering *Kluane* through this storm," Dad's voice carried above the wind. "These swells are so high that if we surf down the wave in the wrong direction, we could easily flip *Kluane* over. Hand steering will give us more control. Let's take two-hour shifts at the helm. Managing the sails is also going to be a chore. We'll need enough sail area to give us power to maintain direction, but not so much sail that we are out of control. Pamela, while I'm at the helm, you're going to have to keep a close watch on the sails."

The waves tossed Sam around all over his bunk. Sleep would be difficult; the storm seemed to be getting worse.

Knowing that his parents would be up all night long upset him even more. He could hear them both curse whenever a wave crashed over *Kluane*, leaving them drenched in salt water. They would be wearing their heavy-duty rain gear for protection from the water, but somehow the water would still penetrate inside the clothing.

As the night wore on, the storm did not subside. Howling winds — up to forty-five knots — continued to haunt them. *Kluane* knocked about continuously, sending things flying about the cabin no matter how securely stored. One knock on *Kluane*'s hull broke the latch on the binocular cabinet and sent the binoculars straight across the cabin into the galley sink.

Sam lay quietly in his sleeping bag, secretly wondering if he would survive the night. Never before had he been so frightened. As much as he wanted to say it aloud, he knew he had to keep his thoughts to himself. His parents had enough worries just managing *Kluane*.

The constant motion made it too difficult to sleep in their bunks, so the boys moved once more into the main cabin bunks with their lee cloths raised to hold them in place. It helped a little; they didn't bounce around as much. But as for sleep . . . impossible.

Morning seemed to take forever to come. At times through the night, Sam was able to doze, but this was always abruptly interrupted by another wave crashing over *Kluane*. By the time morning arrived, Sam felt he had personally climbed each forty-foot swell and fallen down the other side. He was exhausted.

But regardless of how bad the storm could get, it always seemed easier to cope in the daylight. The winds continued to howl, and the sea remained wild, but at least Sam was free of the fears that night brought. Still, the sky showed no sign of hope. *Kluane* was pitching about so much that Sam had to hold on for dear life just to stand up. He realized they were safer in their bunks. When Charlie finally woke from his sleep, Sam had assembled a collection of games and art supplies for both of them.

"Good morning boys," announced Mom, once she had time to notice that they were both awake. "I think you're best to stay in your bunks all day because it's too dangerous to even walk around. I'm afraid that I can't do any cooking until the seas are calmer, so if you want any food, you'll have to resort to granola bars and fruit. I'm not sure how long this storm will last but we'll have to make do whatever way we can."

Sam had never seen his mom look so awful. She was exhausted and very serious. Today I will have to take good care of Charlie, Sam thought. If only the storm would stop.

"I just want to call a taxi," Mom cried from the cockpit later. "Oh, wouldn't it be wonderful to be going out for lunch with the girls today. Michael, I just want to go home . . . but I can't go home because we no longer have one. Please let this storm end soon! This is the greatest endurance test I have ever had."

Dad sounded exhausted. "I know. If this is sailing, then maybe I'm not cut out for it after all. I'm sorry, but I never thought it would be this bad."

Sam's heart sank. He had never heard his parents talk this way. Even Mom, who was always so positive about everything, seemed lower than she had ever been.

The ocean passage to Tonga was supposed to take three days. But the headwinds were too strong, and *Kluane* continued to tack. At the end of three days, they were still a long way from Tonga. The storm showed no signs of letting up. The boys had no choice but to stay in their bunks and be patient. Sometimes Mom had to give them medicine that would lightly sedate them so they could relax and get some sleep.

It was the worst test of discomfort they had ever faced. They barely slept or ate for the entire three days. The cabin was a dreadful mess, with everything strewn about and dampened by salt water. All hatches had to be tightly closed to prevent salt water from seeping below each time a wave crashed over *Kluane*, so there was no fresh air in the cabin, and it smelled stale.

Mom and Dad spent each endless day huddled in their heavy rain gear near the cabin hatchway in the cockpit, barely managing to stay awake and keep *Kluane* in order. Suddenly, one afternoon they heard a strange noise from inside the cabin — a sound they hadn't heard for many days — a laughing sound.

Sure enough, Sam and Charlie had made a game out of the situation by selecting any object that would be a great "flyer," and seeing where it landed as *Kluane* tossed about.

"We are going to have quite a mess to clean up when we get into port, but at least you're having fun," said Mom. "Be very careful of what you use as your flying objects."

On the fourth day, the winds subsided enough to let Sam and Charlie out of their bunks. The seas were still rough and the sky still had a nasty look, but the winds finally calmed down to thirty-five knots. Mom and Dad were far too exhausted to feel happy about anything, but at least there would be hope of getting to Tonga soon.

"How can you tell what the weather will be like just by looking at the sky, Dad?" asked Charlie.

"I think Sam can tell you that, if he looks it up and shows you," Dad answered tiredly. "Maybe today would be a good day to make up another report."

"Sure, Dad." Sam swallowed a protest and put his arm around Charlie as they headed back to the main cabin. "You can give me a hand drawing the clouds, Charlie," he said.

Predicting Weather

by

Sam and Charlie Bendall

When we are trying to predict weather for sailing, we examine three main items: clouds, fog, and wind. Clouds give us clues about approaching weather. They appear in many shapes, but there are really only three main forms — cirrus, cumulus and stratus. Those shapes are important for determining exactly what kind of weather to expect, and even how long it will take before that weather arrives. Here's a drawing of those three shapes:

Stratus Clouds
(stray-tuss)
Low and spread out in layers

May become dark and thick
– Will bring rain

Cirrus Clouds
(sir-us)
Very high and wispy

When they look like horse tails
A storm is approaching

Cumulus Clouds
(Coom-you-lass)
Puffy and white

When they pile up and get dark a storm is coming.

Clouds are formed from an accumulation of tiny bits of moisture in the air, which we call vapour. This vapour rises from the earth, which is warm, to meet the colder air from above and joins together with other water droplets in the air to form cloud masses. This is called condensing. Fog is a cloud that lies close to the ground. If you blow warm air out of your mouth on a cold day, you can make your own little cloud.

Clouds don't make the wind. Wind is formed by an exchange of air. The air at the earth's surface gets heated by the sun and warms the air nearby, which rises and is replaced by cooler air. That exchange of warm air rising and cool air descending is what creates wind.

Charlie looked up from his task of colouring the clouds. "A weatherman has a pretty interesting job. Maybe I'll become a weatherman when I grow up."

By the time *Kluane* approached the Tongan shores, there was no energy left in anyone for excitement. The previous five days had been gruelling. Sam had never seen his parents in such a bad state. The experience had completely dampened their enthusiasm for sailing. Sam even heard them talking about selling *Kluane* if an opportunity arose.

August 25
Dear Tristan,

We made it! The waves are still a little crazy but nothing like the past few days. The Tongan shoreline looks beautiful, with high cliffs everywhere. The porpoises have come to greet us again, but this time Mom doesn't seem to have the energy to get the video going. You should see Kluane. *She looks like she is coming home from war — inside and out. I hope we never have to go through anything like those last five days again . . . for the rest of my life!!!*

Mom called the Tonga customs station on our VHF radio to tell them that we're coming. Right after she finished with them, guess who called us back? Venture!!! *They must have left Samoa just after us, but because* Venture *is a bigger boat, they were able to get here earlier. Dick said they also had an awful passage. I hope that we can see them again when we get into port.*

Almost as soon as *Kluane*'s anchor was down, Dick arrived by dinghy with a surprise that immediately lifted everyone's spirits — three full bags of treats. Ice cream, cookies, spaghetti sauce, fresh bread, ice, and some very cold beer for Mom and Dad. Perhaps sailing wasn't so bad after all, thought Sam, even if it does mean being brave at times.

It took five solid days of cleaning to bring *Kluane* back into proper shape after her arrival. When they weren't helping, Sam and Charlie spent their time swimming and playing at the Paradise Hotel, which sat right in front of *Kluane*'s anchorage.

August 30
Dear Tristan,

This is the first day that Mom is able to get off Kluane *and begin exploring. She has had to wash down every part of the boat, including all the pillows and cushions. Everything got soaked in that passage. We have been swimming all day long in the pool, but now I'm ready to see what Tonga is about.*

I looked up a few facts about Tonga for you. Did you know it is the only kingdom left in the Pacific Islands? There are over sixty islands, all sitting like a chain running north to south over 350 miles. The king has his grand Royal Palace in the capital city of Nuku'alofa, which is located in the south of the chain. In the year 1900, Tonga became an independent country. Tonga is a protectorate of Britain. That means Britain keeps an eye on Tonga, Dad says.

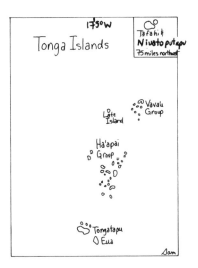

One of the first things that Sam and Charlie noticed as they climbed the hill going towards town, was a tapping noise coming from the village. It sounded like a whole bunch of people hammering something. Their curiosity took over, and before long the boys had convinced their parents to investigate. Sam led the way, following the noise until he finally came upon a Tongan home, with women sitting on the floors pounding something with wodden mallets.

"Could you please explain to us what you are doing?" Sam asked the lady with the friendliest face.

"We are making tapa cloth," she said in broken English, with a huge smile on her face. "We take the bark from mulberry tree and tap it with hammers until we have long sheets. Then, we tap the sheets together to make one big tapa cloth. After that we use dyes from our plants to make designs. These are sometimes symbols of the village where we live."

Charlie and Sam couldn't believe the women could make such impressive creations from the bark of a tree. How could they sit on that cabin floor, day after day, doing the same task in such noisy conditions?

The rest of the tour took them through the market and the centre of town. A friendly man named Mutotu approached them at the market and kindly invited the family to a true Tongan feast in his village. The family eagerly accepted the invitation and thanked Mutotu for his kindness. Mutotu also offered to bring fresh market vegetables from his village to *Kluane* each day during their stay.

And he did. Every day, from that time on, Mutotu came by *Kluane* in his dugout canoe at approximately the same time. He brought carvings, fruit, tapa cloth, and fresh vegetables. Plans were made for the feast in his village the following Friday evening.

Sam finally realized what the word "feast" really meant when he saw all the food arrive. Long trays made from banana leaves were covered with an incredible selection of Tongan specialties, which neither Sam nor Charlie had ever dreamed of eating: dog meat, horse, stuffed octopus, along with every variety of fish.

Everyone sat on the floor of the hut and ate with their fingers. Sam was impressed because not one item of food nor one serving utensil came from a store. Every food, wrapping, and serving dish was handmade by the local women. Better still, Sam and Charlie had never eaten so much delicious food. The boys ate until they couldn't fit another morsel into their stomachs.

When the feast and speeches were over, Sam and Charlie thanked Mutotu for the tremendous experience and gave him a donation from their savings. The donation would go towards something useful in the village, because few people in Tonga had true jobs or could earn money.

September 10

Dear Tristan,

I really like it here in Tonga, but also can't wait to go to Fiji. Mom just registered us in a yacht regatta (that means a race) in Fiji, which begins in three weeks, so now I think we are going to cut our stay in Tonga short and leave tomorrow so we can be at the regatta in time.

Dick and Nancy on Venture *are our best friends. They are so nice to us. It's almost as though they are our grandparents, because they seem to really care.* Venture *has a VCR on board, and they sometimes ask Charlie and me to come over and watch a movie. I think we'll see them again in Fiji — hope so.*

We also met some really nice people from a Mexican boat named Pegaso *— she is sixty feet long and even has a washer and dryer, along with lots of neat stuff. All our friends seem to be adults, but I think that's the sailing life. Herta and George on* Pegaso *seem to really like kids and always welcome us on board.*

Mom is being crazy again. A boat named Canada Goose *(from Australia) is leaving for Fiji the same time as us, so Mom has organized a race with them. The first boat to Fiji gets a free round of drinks at the Royal Suva Yacht Club when we arrive.* Canada Goose *is three feet longer than* Kluane *and has more crew than us so they'll probably win. But if I know my mom, it won't be easy. She's a very competitive person. I hope this passage isn't bad like the last one. Dad calculates that it will take us three days to get there and says it should be downwind and calm the entire way . . . but I've heard that one before . . .*

10.   A Close Call

Kluane was able to clear Tongan customs before *Canada Goose*, which was just the head start she needed. The two yachts had pre-arranged radio calls scheduled twice daily throughout the race for safety, and recording their progress.

"If we can just keep these perfect wind conditions for the rest of the passage, we'll clean up in the race," said Mom gleefully. "*Canada Goose* may be a bigger boat with more crew, but *Kluane* is at her best in twenty-five knot winds with the wind direction just on her beam. I think we have a fighting chance."

Something had possessed Mom, Sam thought. Something had changed her from the mom who wanted to sell the boat and give up sailing forever. Of course Sam was glad of it, he told himself, but still it was a little weird to see her like this.

Almost as if she had been reading his thoughts, Mom suddenly turned and looked at Sam. "These seas are so calm, you'll be able to do your school work on this passage. Why don't you get started so that you can have more free time in Fiji?"

Sam groaned. His first yacht race, and he'd be below in a tie. Life wasn't fair, he told himself, and he reluctantly hauled himself below to get his books.

"Kluane, Kluane, Kluane," called *Canada Goose* over the VHF radio.

Immediately Mom was below with the transmitter in her hand. "This is Kluane," she replied. "How are you and what is your position now?"

"We have just lost sight of land. It took us two hours to clear Tongan customs so I expect that we are roughly two hours behind you now."

"Okay Canada Goose, we have that recorded. If everything else is fine on board, we'll say goodnight and catch you on the airwaves at seven tomorrow morning. Say 'hi' to everyone on Canada Goose. Kluane clear."

By morning, *Canada Goose* was still well behind *Kluane*. The sail was so pleasant in comparison to any other passage, it was hard to even think of racing. Everyone just wanted to relax and enjoy it. Even Charlie seemed glad of the smooth ride.

"This is the first time that I have actually been able to drink a cup of coffee in the cockpit without fear that it's going to spill everywhere when the next wave hits," said Mom.

"Yes," Dad agreed, laughing. "I think we have had nothing but bad luck with weather on our ocean passages. I heard on the radio yesterday that the University of Hawaii claims that El Nino has caused tremendous changes in weather patterns this year in the Pacific. That could account for our inconsistent currents and winds throughout the Pacific."

"Who is El Nino?" asked Charlie innocently.

"El Nino means 'little child,' which refers to the Christ child," Dad answered. "They call it that because El Nino usually comes in December. It's a very warm current of water."

"Well, he came pretty early this year," answered Charlie emphatically.

September 13
Dear Tristan,

This race is so exciting! Canada Goose is just behind us with less than one hundred miles to go. We should arrive in Fiji at sunrise tomorrow morning, so Mom is going crazy trying to make sure we win. I think Dad is letting her take over as skipper because he doesn't care about the race — maybe only the prize. She insists on hand steering now because it's a little more efficient and the race is so close. I hope we win so that she is not disappointed.

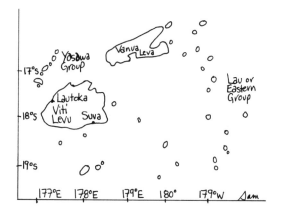

That night, on the scheduled radio call, it appeared that *Canada Goose* was about to take over the lead. The winds had lowered to fifteen knots, giving the longer boat the advantage. Sam could not believe his ears when he heard that *Canada Goose* was gaining such speed.

"Isn't there anything we can do to catch up?" he asked. "C'mon Mom, don't let them get ahead now! Hey, Dad, you're the skipper, now's your chance to prove your sailing skills."

Dad laughed. "Sorry, Son. Sailing can be frustrating at times, because you just don't have control over the weather. You never know though, things could change during the night."

At ten p.m. *Canada Goose* made a final call to *Kluane*, advising that their expected time of arrival of the bigger boat into Suva would be two a.m. Mom and Dad estimated that *Kluane* wouldn't make it until six a.m. It appeared that *Canada Goose* would be the winner.

Mom could barely suppress her disappointment. "Congratulations, and have a safe arrival. We'll look forward to seeing you in port," she said.

But as *Kluane* approached Suva Harbour, fully expecting to see *Canada Goose* secured safely in port, Sam couldn't believe his eyes. The bigger boat was wallowing outside the harbour entrance. Sam grabbed the binoculars and peered through them. Sure enough, it was *Canada Goose* passively waiting for their arrival. He passed the binoculars to Mom, who took a quick look before she ran to the radio.

"Canada Goose, Canada Goose, Canada Goose, please come in," Mom called.

"Good morning Kluane, and welcome to Fiji." The voice at the other end sounded a little glum. "We did arrive here at approximately two a.m., but when we tried to start the engine, it wouldn't turn over. It's unsafe to try to enter this busy harbour at night without an engine, so we were hoping that you wouldn't mind giving us a tow?"

"Well, as you know, we are always happy to lend a hand, but you also know what that means," replied Mom jokingly. "If we are towing you, then *Kluane* will enter the harbour before *Canada Goose*, so guess who the official winners will be?"

A hoot of laughter greeted her remark. "Well Kluane, maybe we can strike a deal."

It didn't take long for both yachts to agree that, under the circumstances, *Kluane* and *Canada Goose* had tied in the race. As the bigger boat hitched a ride behind them, Sam realized that, for the first time since they had left Canada, they were arriving into port feeling fresh and relaxed.

September 14
Dear Tristan,

We are in Suva, Fiji, now. It looks like it's going to be quite similar to the other islands we have visited in the South Pacific except that Suva is much larger and busier. Dad plans to buy all sorts of equipment for the boat here because it's the cheapest place in the Pacific. And we're finally going to get the Sat Nav fixed!

The only thing I don't like about Fiji so far is all the military people. Mom told me that Fiji is made up of Fijians and East Indian people. The Fijians and East Indians are having a hard time here because the Fijians think that the East Indians are taking over. Fijian military men are everywhere, and carry these huge rifles. I told Charlie he'd better be careful 'cause he doesn't want to do anything wrong here!

Mom says that there was a coup here in May. They had an election, and the East Indians got more seats in the government, so the Fijians got angry and decided to take over the government. I think the Fijians are nervous that if the Indians have too much control, then Fiji will lose its special Fijian culture. I can see why there's a fight, because many of the Indians have been here for several generations. It feels like home to them too. They work very hard to keep all the shops and businesses running, which really helps Fiji's economy. I can see both sides. I just hope that there's no more fighting — at least until we leave.

We are only staying in Suva a little while, and then heading to the regatta at Malololailai Island. Charlie and I have been practising saying Malololailai, and now that's all he says . . . Malololailai, Malololailai . . . it drives me crazy!

The first week in Suva seemed to go by in a flash. Sam and Charlie met a number of sailing kids at the Suva Yacht Club and played with them every day. Sam and Charlie had become used to each other's company, but it was a treat to play with a gang of other kids again. Mom and Dad were busy preparing *Kluane* for the final two months of sailing before they'd reach New Zealand. Fijian prices were so much cheaper than anywhere else that the purchase of a single-side band radio made a lot of sense. With a single-side band *Kluane* could then be reached by radio from anywhere in the world. Mom and Dad seemed visibly relieved at the thought of having it on board. Their marine radio only worked for short-range calls. It was hard to count the number of times they could have used a single-side band, Sam thought.

September 17
Dear Tristan,

We are going on a hike today and I have asked a girl to come. Don't get me wrong, Jade is just a friend — it's not her fault she's a girl. We get along really well. Jade and her family are from Arizona and are sailing on a eighty-three foot boat named Moblue. *It's huge!*

She has long, blond hair, and she's really smart — not the kind of blond that can't do anything. In fact, I think Jade might be able to run faster than me. I know she can climb better than me, because she is always climbing up the boat's halyards and shrouds — you wouldn't catch me doing that. More than anything else though, Jade is just a really nice friend and we always have fun together. I can't wait to go on this hike with her. Mom says that at the end of the hike we'll find some beautiful swimming pools and a waterfall. Do you have a girl friend yet? I mean the kind of friend who just happens to be a girl.

The hiking trip was a huge success. A jeep took them up the mountainside to the spot where the path began. Then, single file, the family followed the path, which led them through the steep jungle terrain. When they finally arrived at the swimming pools, a large crowd of local Fijian teenagers were playing in the water. They had built a swing rope over the swimming hole so they could swing from several different rock ledges at various heights around the pools and then drop down into the water hole.

The Fijian boys were the most daring group Sam had ever seen. Everyone watched their show with fascination, clapping as each Fijian attempted higher and higher feats.

"Hey, that looks like fun!" cried Jade. "I'll see you later Sam." And before Sam could say "you've got to be crazy," Jade had climbed to the highest platform, handled by only the most skilled Fijian teenagers. She held her hand out, requesting the rope. Suddenly the crowd below was silent. The spectators held their breath as they watched Jade with intense interest. Could this young ten-year-old girl manage a feat that even the older local boys had difficulty with?

Mom tugged at Dad's arm. "Michael, I wonder if we should stop Jade — after all, we are responsible for her," Mom said. Sam didn't know whether to be excited or worried, but he never took his eyes off Jade for one second. What an incredible girl, he thought. She was crazy.

Without hesitation, Jade swung into the air and splashed down into the water with the grace of an eagle. When she surfaced, every spectator in the area cheered. Jade seemed surprised, as if she couldn't figure out why everyone was so excited about something so easy.

"C'mon Sam, it's easy, give it a try."

There was no way that Sam was going to back down from a challenge offered by a girl. He climbed to the highest platform.

As he stood at the top and looked down, his body began to shake. The swimming hole below seemed a mile away, and Charlie was the size of a pea. Then, as Sam looked around, he suddenly noticed that all of the spectators' eyes were now glued on him. No one spoke. The crowd was so still, they looked like tiny statues in a wax museum.

He had two choices. He could either jump off the ledge quickly and hope he didn't die, or die of embarrassment by climbing down the bank and giving up. No doubt about it, the first choice was the better one.

Sam took a big breath, whispered "one, two, three — go," and was off the ledge. He hit the water with a shattering impact, surfaced quickly and looked around. He was still alive. The crowd roared their approval. Sam and Jade became instant heroes, and spent the rest of the afternoon swinging from platforms at every level.

Exactly one week after their arrival in Fiji, Dad came home from the morning's shopping trip, his face drained of its usual dark tan.

"Prepare *Kluane* to leave port immediately," he ordered. "There's a coup taking place in Suva, and the city's been closed. It's not safe to be here. If we leave now, we can be in Malololailai by dark tomorrow night. Sam, help me haul in the anchor; Pamela, get everything in order below."

No one argued as they sprang into action. When he cast off, Sam took a last look over his shoulder. Huge clouds of smoke billowed over the city skyline. No noise, no panic, just smoke. But it was enough. Sam ran below to help Mom and Charlie stow their things. *Kluane* was just one of many boats instantly departing Suva Harbour. A huge trail of yachts followed each other out to sea that afternoon, leaving Suva and her political troubles behind.

Once they were under way and everyone could relax a little, Dad filled them in on the details. He had spent the morning shopping in downtown Suva — just like any other day. But at approximately noon, the entire city instantly turned into turmoil. Riots broke out right before his eyes, with guns fired all around him and huge explosions of smoke in the streets ahead. It was chaos everywhere, with people running in all directions in absolute panic. Dad immediately forgot about what he was shopping for and hopped into the nearest taxi.

"Take me to the Suva Yacht Club please, and fast," he told the driver.

"We just heard over the taxi station radio that the military has ordered the city closed," replied the driver. "We have another coup like the one in May. You are best to leave this place completely if you want to be safe. I'll take you to the yacht club, but after that I'm not doing any more rides."

Dad finished his story. For a moment no one said anything. Then Charlie put his hand on Dad's shoulder and grinned. "Pretty close call, eh Dad?"

11. *Kluane* Survives Another Test

Malololailai Island in Western Fiji was everything the family hoped for after their hasty retreat from Suva. The island was a small tropical paradise, surrounded by coral reefs where visitors could spend the day snorkelling and scuba diving. Over forty boats from every corner of the world were anchored in the bay, all ready for Regatta Week.

Sam and Charlie rarely saw their parents during Regatta Week. All day, every day, they played with new exciting friends and took part in regatta activities. Sam and Charlie loved having so many kids to play with, and Sam found that he could leave his brother with a group his own age. Sam's three best friends were Brent (on the boat *Tahiti Maz*) from Australia, Jocie, whose parents owned Malololailai Island, and of course, Jade.

One of the sailing races took the regatta yachts to a nearby spot called Beachcomber Island. They all had a glorious day playing about and exploring this new island.

In fact, the place was so much fun, no one realized how late it had become. When Mom finally called the boys in, her voice had a no-nonsense tone that didn't permit argument.

"Why did we have to get going so soon?" asked Charlie, as they headed back to Malololailai. "It's just afternoon and won't be dark for a long time. Besides, we sail at night all the time, right?"

"The danger of sailing in these waters is that coral reefs are everywhere and they lie just below the water's surface," answered

Dad from the helm. "We have to be careful and only navigate the area when the sun is high above, because the coral is hard to see otherwise. The reefs are sharp enough to sink a boat, certainly sharp enough to do some major damage."

Dark clouds hovered over *Kluane* as she turned into Malololailai Island, so it was impossible for the crew to see any reefs below. Sam and a visiting crew member stood on the bow deck checking for any signs of coral as they motored up the channel.

Suddenly, with a horrible crash, *Kluane* came to a full stop. She hit a reef head on! Sam ran back to the cockpit to help his Dad.

"Sam, find Charlie and Mom, make sure they're all right," Dad said as he tried to back up, off the reef.

Moving quickly, Sam found Charlie on his bunk, mouth open in astonishment. In the main cabin he found Mom on the floor in a complete daze. She had been knocked out in the crash.

"Quick Dad!" he called, as he crouched over her. "Mom is hurt! She's lying on the floor in the galley."

But Dad had his hands full, checking the bilges below the floorboards to see that no water was leaking inside. So far, no great damage had resulted from the crash, but the problem still remained that they were sitting on top of a reef. Severe damage could still result if they didn't act quickly.

"Dad! Mom is in bad shape. I think she's unconscious," Sam pleaded. Just then, Sam noticed his mom's eyes begin to move. She seemed surprised to find herself lying on the galley floor, but smiled to assure Sam that she was all right.

"You should see your face, Mom," Sam couldn't help but laugh. "It's covered in soap suds."

"I was washing the dishes," she answered. "I guess my face landed in the suds before I fell."

Still in a daze, Mom was on her feet within seconds. She joined Dad, and together they tried to assess what could be done. The biggest fear of anyone sailing in the South Pacific was hitting a reef. Darkness was quickly approaching, and if *Kluane* couldn't get to safety soon, they were in serious trouble. They must find a way to release *Kluane* from the reef quickly.

After a quick consultation, Dad managed to pull the boom to one side of *Kluane*.

"Okay everyone, climb on top!" he shouted.

The crew obeyed without hesitation, as they scrambled onto the boom and held on as best they could. Finally, with so much weight on one side, *Kluane* heeled over and was freed from the reef.

Dad cried from the helm, "We're off! Stay there for a second while I back us up."

A minute later, they were headed on the proper course. But by now it was so dark, that Mom radioed to Malololailai Island for assistance into the island bay. Dick Smith, the owner of the resort on the beach, arrived in his speed boat in a flash and led *Kluane* to safety.

"Boy, I have never been so scared in my life," exclaimed Sam. "I thought it was over for us. Dad, you were brilliant."

Dad shook his head. "We were very lucky, Sammy."

"Hey, where's Mom?" asked Charlie.

"I'm in the galley cleaning up the mess," she called. "There's a huge bump on my forehead, but that's the only visible damage down here. Boy, I sure learned a lesson today — never do the dishes when you're heading up a channel!"

The very next day, Dad and several scuba divers dove below to check *Kluane*'s hull for any damage. Sam and Charlie watched intently as the divers donned their tanks and regulators. Fifteen minutes went by — the longest fifteen minutes ever.

Finally, when the divers surfaced, they had the best news. The coral had scratched a tiny mark on the keel, but *Kluane* had escaped serious damage.

"Chalk up another victory for *Kluane*," said Mom. "Yet another test she has survived brilliantly."

One of the scuba divers noticed that Charlie was particularly interested in all the diving gear, so he began showing Charlie the various pieces of equipment. The diver held the diving tank, and Charlie swam on the surface of the water in his life jacket while he used the diving regulator.

"Hey, Sam," he shouted as he was pulled back on deck. "You won't believe what I saw down there! I saw every kind of fish you can imagine. Big fish too. If I become a biologist when I grow up, I'm going to be a scuba diver and learn about fish."

"That's called a marine biologist son," said the diver. "You would make a great marine biologist. You would learn all about marine life."

"Yup, that's exactly what I'll do," said Charlie. "That's the best job I can think of. I'll be able to swim and look at fish all day long!"

Kluane's reef encounter became the "talk of the bay" for the rest of the week. One positive result of the adventure was the popularity the boys suddenly enjoyed. Everywhere they went, Sam and Charlie had the chance to tell their versions of the story, which got more and more exciting each time they told them.

And when the Talent Contest Night arrived, *Kluane*'s crew could only think of . . . a skit by the "Kluane Reefers," performed to the tune of "On Top of Old Smokey." Sam and Charlie were dressed like two of the Three Blind Mice and helped compose a skit highlighting the events of the reef encounter. Though their nerves were frazzled by show time, their skit was a success. They won a special prize — dinner for the entire family in the resort's very expensive restaurant.

"I just can't believe we won the prize," Sam repeated over and over. "Sometimes bad experiences can lead to positive ones."

The final day of the regatta was the most special. All boats prepared for the "Live Figurehead Parade," when every boat was elaborately decorated in the finest style possible. A huge parade would take place in the afternoon as each boat would circle around the bay and be judged for the grandest prize of all.

Sam's and Brent's parents decided that both families would work together, decorating *Tahiti Maz* for the contest. Sam, Charlie, and Brent spent the morning collecting palm boughs from the shore. Soon they had enough boughs to decorate the entire deck of *Tahiti Maz*, and the dinghy too. The children decided to spend their energy on the dinghy and let the parents concentrate on the big boat. By mid-afternoon, *Tahiti Maz* was beautiful. She was adorned with Fijian-style elegance that captured the hearts of every spectator. Each parent had prepared a traditional grass skirt for the occasion, and several of the local Fijian women offered to come aboard to play authentic Fijian music during the parade.

"But we still have one problem," said Dad, as he secured the last palm bough to the deck. "This parade is called a 'Live Figurehead Parade.' We can't expect to win the prize unless we have something special as a figurehead, right on the bow. Pamela, you were once a gymnast, why don't you do a handstand on the bowsprit?"

"Very funny, Michael," Mom answered. "You're forgetting that a few years have passed since my gymnast days. I know I could do the handstand, but I would have to hold it for the entire parade!"

"You're not admitting to me that you're getting old, are

you?'' Dad continued, winking at Sam.

"C'mon Mom, you can do it," Sam pursued. "We've done so much work on the parade now, you've got to at least try."

"Okay, I'll try. But I can't guarantee any results."

Sam couldn't believe his eyes as the parade began and all the boats took formation into one line. *Tahiti Maz* proudly filed into line with Sam, Charlie, and Brent trailing behind in *Kluane II Too.* They were just one of many yachts in the bay, elaborately adorned in every way he could imagine.

He peered forward to the bowsprit and saw his mom upside down in a handstand, holding on for dear life. As the boats continued to parade around the bay, the seas became choppy and disorderly.

"How much longer do I have to stay up here?" Sam heard his mother cry. "My shoulders are getting weak, and it's really hard to balance with all this chop. Besides, I can't see the parade!"

"Hang in there Pamela, it'll be over soon," Dad called. Fortunately, he was right. One second later, and Mom definitely would have collapsed.

The end of the parade marked a very sad moment for Sam. Until then, he really hadn't paid attention to the fact that tomorrow was departure day for many boats. The regatta events were now officially finished, and he would have to face saying good-bye to many of his special friends. Brent would be returning to Australia, and they would probably never see each other again. Jocie would always live at Malololailai, and when would they ever get back here? The only salvation was that Jade would be going to New Zealand too. Sam knew that their parents had become quite close, so he and Jade would see each other again.

Malololailai Resort was alive that night as everyone

extended their final greetings to each other, and made plans for the future. The week-long regatta provided special memories for every sailor there, together with intense friendships that would never be forgotten. Sam and Brent exchanged addresses and promised to write to each other, yet Sam couldn't help but feel saddened by the thought that he was losing his closest male friend.

"Good evening, sailors," announced the resort owner, Dick Smith. "We have some very special awards to present this evening."

Sam listened intently as Dick Smith began handing out the prizes for the "Live Figurehead" contest. Sam knew that the prize for first place was a hand-held marine radio — something he had always dreamed of having. When the last three top placings were announced, Sam's heart began to pound faster and faster. He tried not to get too excited. He knew how disappointed he would feel if they didn't win.

"And the first place prize goes to *Tahiti Maz* — winners of the Live Figurehead contest!" Dick Smith's announcement sent shock waves through Sam's entire body.

"We won!" they all cried in unison, cheering as they went to receive their prize. Since there were two families and only one radio, Sam's dad agreed to take cash value from Brent's dad and use the money to buy a ham single-side band marine radio.

Instead of leaving for New Zealand the next day, *Kluane* would head back to Lautoka, a major city in Western Fiji, and buy their new radio.

Sam was awakened the following morning by a knock on the hull. He ran outside as quickly as he could, then suddenly stopped when he realized what was happening. Brent and his parents had arrived to say their final farewells. Now, Sam would have to face that dreaded moment. There had only been one good male friend in Sam's life since he left Glenlyon School last May. Chances were very remote that another friend like Brent would appear soon. The boys shook hands, promised to write letters often, and then parted quickly before their emotions began to show. Sam watched *Tahiti Maz* sail away into the horizon and then escaped into his cabin to fight back his tears.

September 29
Dear Tristan,

I'm glad you're here. This week was so much fun, and suddenly it's over. I really miss having a good friend like you. Charlie and my folks are nice, but it's not the same as having a friend the same age. Thank heavens Jade is still here because she's lots of fun.

Pretty soon we'll be heading to Lautoka to buy loads of new things — a single-side band marine radio, four horsepower outboard motor for the dinghy, and some new clothes for New Zealand. We have hardly worn clothes for the last six months, and know that New Zealand will be cold. Mom says that everything in New Zealand is really expensive so we're going to get as much as possible here.

Thanks for listening, I feel better already.

Another week passed before *Kluane* and her crew were fully prepared for the next ocean passage to New Zealand. This would be their last voyage for many months, as the family intended to stay in New Zealand for at least half a year.

Sam used the week in Lautoka to catch up on his school work, which had been somewhat neglected during their week in Malololailai. He had only one more assignment to finish in his first semester. That meant he would be one-third of the way through grade five. So every day was spent doing school work, while his parents and Charlie went shopping in town.

October 9
Dear Tristan,

Mom, Dad, and Charlie just left for Lautoka, and once again I'm here on Kluane supposedly doing my school work. Sometimes I really wish I had a proper teacher. I know that I'm lucky to be doing correspondence, but sometimes I get really frustrated with Mom. She always seems to be at me. Clean the decks, keep my cabin tidy, look after Charlie, do watch, do the dishes. And if it's not that stuff, she's at me about school work. It's not easy having your mom as a teacher.

Dad says that he's bringing home a new outboard motor for Kluane II Too today. If he gets the four horsepower, we'll be able to plane in the dinghy. Hope they get home soon.

Guess I better get my work done now. See ya.

Sam couldn't believe his eyes when the family returned to *Kluane.* "Wow, look at all this stuff," he cried.

"Hey Sam, we got a new radio that lets us talk to people anywhere in the world — right from the middle of the ocean!" exclaimed Charlie, as he pulled out the pamphlet and handed it to Sam. "And we also got an electronic keyboard that plays five different instruments. And some new clothes, even."

"Fantastic!" cried Sam. "Look at all this stuff. This is better than Christmas."

All the gear was quickly stowed and last-minute provisions loaded onto *Kluane.* Weather reports indicated that the time was right to set off for New Zealand.

"If we work hard today, we should be able to clear through customs late this afternoon and head out early tomorrow morning," announced Dad. "Pamela, you look after the food and the inside cabin, I'll try to get this new equipment fitted. This next passage to New Zealand has a reputation of being brutal, so we want to make sure that we take advantage of good weather conditions."

12. We Made It!

Dad had only one job to complete before *Kluane*'s departure for New Zealand early in the morning, on October 10. He had to be sure that the new single-side band radio antenna was receiving signals.

"Pamela, are you getting any signals yet?" he hollered from the cockpit.

"No, Michael, nothing," she answered, as she dialled every frequency available on the airwaves.

Suddenly, a very familiar voice filled the cabin. "Kluane, Kluane, Kluane, this is Venture. Do you copy?"

"Venture, Venture, Venture, I copy you loud and clear. Please give me your position and itinerary."

"We are leaving today for New Zealand, along with *Pegaso* and *Sylvia*. We hope you will be joining us soon."

Sam and Charlie raised their fists in the air. "All right!"

Mom laughed as she put her finger to her lips in an effort to quiet them. "Venture, in fact we are leaving today. Let's have a race and make this passage even more exciting. How about a handicap of one day for every ten feet of boat length since all the boats are different sizes."

"Kluane, do I read you correctly? If *Pegaso*, which is sixty-five feet, arrives in New Zealand in six days, then *Venture*, at forty-five feet, could still win if we get there before eight days?"

"That's correct. And *Kluane* can still win even if we arrive last."

The details were set. They agreed to meet on their single-side band radio twice daily at pre-arranged times to give positions and relay any messages.

New Zealand. It had been Mom and Dad's dream for many years, Sam and Charlie's dream for the past two years as well. This crossing marked the last leg of their journey. Sam couldn't imagine what would follow; it seemed as if they had lived nowhere else but on *Kluane*.

Strangely enough, the ocean passage that they feared the most turned out to be the easiest. The winds were consistently twenty-five knots from behind, with an average speed of seven and one-half knots. *Kluane* flew along, gaining over 150 miles each day. It was almost as if she knew that the end was near, Sam thought.

Sam had the job of charting each yacht's position. The radio calls twice daily offered lots of excitement; *Pegaso* immediately took the lead, with *Sylvia* second, followed by *Venture*, then *Kluane*. The ultimate winner would remain in question until the end, when the handicap system would be evaluated. As he marked each boat's position, Sam studied the distance between them. It was impossible to tell who was ahead, but even if *Kluane* was winning the race, Sam hated to mark her position behind the bigger boats.

A few days later, as Sam and Charlie were sitting quietly on the bow watching the waves break against the hull, a strange sound from the cabin below caught their attention.

"Hey, Charlie, listen; Mom and Dad are fighting. Come on. I want to hear this."

Both boys crept closer to the hatchway to listen.

"You're the only person in this world who can spend money at sea!" they heard Dad yell. "You're impossible."

Sam and Charlie couldn't believe their ears. They crawled

right into the cockpit to hear more.

"But Michael," Mom answered, "I really didn't know it would cost so much. I was simply trying to figure out this new radio. I thought it would be important to learn how to make a long-distance call in case of an emergency. So I just followed the directions, and before I knew it, I had the overseas operator asking for the number I wished to call. So I followed the instructions and gave her Bill Pearce's number in Canada. Before I knew it, Bill was on the phone. He was pretty excited to hear that we were calling from the middle of the ocean. I had no idea it would cost sixty-eight dollars!"

"Sixty-eight dollars," whispered Sam. "That's half our weekly budget."

"Besides," Mom continued, "aren't you glad to know the radio works?"

Dad's voice sounded weary. "All right, but from now on, only use the overseas operator in an emergency."

October 15
Dear Tristan,

We have been at sea for five days, and so far the trip has been great. If we keep this up, we'll be in New Zealand in two days. Pegaso is almost there already, and Sylvia only has half a day to go. Venture will arrive in New Zealand tomorrow, and we'll get there the day after. Boy, I hope nothing changes and this weather holds out.

Mom has been playing with our new radio a lot. She's calling all the boats around us. It's great, because now we aren't losing track of our friends. And when we say good-bye we can still keep in touch with them. She is also able to talk with weather stations several times every day so we can prepare for bad weather.

Charlie thinks the radio is really neat. He always plays with the radio when Mom's not using it, but only pretends because it's illegal to use it without a licence. Guess what he wants to be now — a radio announcer, what else!

I'm not even seasick this trip. What a relief.

As each day passed, their friends arrived in port on schedule. An award ceremony was planned for the evening after *Kluane*'s arrival, and reservations at a popular restaurant were confirmed for the celebration.

But, only twelve hours and one hundred miles from land, *Kluane*'s fortunes turned sour. Their hope of blissfully sailing into New Zealand came to an abrupt halt when a huge blanket of cloud suddenly descended over the New Zealand coast. Suddenly they had no visibility, and to make matters worse, the Satellite Navigator failed to perform once more. Everything went wrong all at once, leaving *Kluane* and her crew in a very serious situation. In spite of winds gusting to well above forty knots, the blanket of cloud wouldn't disappear.

"I don't like this, Pamela," Dad sounded worried as they desperately peered through the fog. "We're heading directly for an unfamiliar shore, with no visibility or accurate position. We have to slow her down."

Together they took down all but a tiny amount of sail, but *Kluane* barely dropped her frantic speed. And as darkness finally fell, *Kluane* continued to head for land at a speed of more than seven knots. As a last resort, they placed the sails in the "hove to" position and waited until morning in hopes of clear skies.

Occasionally throughout the night Sam would waken to the sounds of his mother calling Kerikeri Radio for assistance. Mom hardly ever called for help from anyone in the middle of the night. Something was very wrong. He could tell from the motion of the boat that they were not moving forward, and he could hear the winds howling through the rigging. *Kluane* bounced around like a cork on the ocean surface. Sam had little sleep that night.

The morning light brought even less hope for the skipper and crew. The thick fog continued to hover over the land mass before them, and by now it was impossible to estimate their position. Mom and Dad stared out at the fog.

"We have no choice, Pamela," Dad finally said. "We know that we're approaching a rugged coastline. We have to turn *Kluane* around and steer a course directly away from land."

"You mean we're not going to see New Zealand today?" Sam wailed. "You told me we would be there this morning. Can't we just wait here until the fog lifts? I don't want to backtrack."

"Sam," Dad answered patiently, "it's the only safe measure considering the fact that our position is not known. You know what they say: 'You're not there until the anchor is down.' We may not get there at all if we take chances."

Kluane's course was altered to 180 degrees away from the New Zealand coast. Now it really appeared that New Zealand was still a dream and nothing more. Sam and Charlie slumped down in their seats in the main cabin. There was nothing to do but wait.

But their friends had not forgotten them. Suddenly a friendly voice crackled over the air waves. "Kluane, Kluane, Kluane," called *Venture*.

Mom leaped to the radio. "Venture, Venture, Venture, this is Kluane, come in please."

"Kluane, we have radar. It is excellent for these conditions, because our radar can locate you despite the fog. I'm leaving

port now and we'll come out and help you find the course into
shore. Stay on this radio frequency, and we'll be there in no time
. . . *Venture* to the rescue!''

"Dick, that's really kind of you, but please don't risk
yourselves for us. We're happy to stay out here until the fog lifts.
It can't stay there forever. Besides, you have already come to our
rescue too often. What would we do without you?''

"We are happy to help, and we won't feel relaxed until we
know you are all safely anchored. That's what this sailing
community is all about. Stay on this frequency and we'll see you
soon. *Venture* clear.''

Just as *Venture* arrived at *Kluane*'s position, the sun
managed to shine faintly through the fog. The crew could finally
see land formations looming out of the distant horizon. At last,
with no fanfare or ceremony, *Venture* safely led the way into the
Bay of Islands — *Kluane*'s home for the next six months.

Sam, Charlie, Mom, and Dad stood quietly on the deck as
Kluane entered the final channel of the entire voyage. All of the
trials, fears, and hardships of the past seven months were quickly
put to rest and replaced with thoughts of how remarkably green
this new discovery appeared.

"It looks a lot like British Columbia, with white speckles,''
cried Sam.

"I think those speckles are sheep, Sam,'' Mom replied.
"Apparently there are over sixty million sheep in this country
and only three million people. I hope you like eating lamb,
because I have a feeling I'll be cooking it often.''

Despite the long delay that *Kluane* encountered coming into
New Zealand, she proudly took first place at the award
ceremony. But more importantly, the ceremony marked another
special occasion — a final gathering of their friends and sailing
companions. After this evening, each of the yachts would be

heading in different directions and would have to say farewell. *Pegaso* was planning to sail west, *Venture* was going east, and *Sylvia* was heading north. *Kluane* was planning to stay in New Zealand for at least another six months, if not longer.

This was the part Sam disliked the most. He hated saying good-bye. The very best thing about this trip had been the people he and Charlie had met. It was hard to imagine not seeing them again.

October 31
Dear Tristan,

It's Halloween today, but no one in New Zealand understands what it is about. Charlie and I plan to dress up and go around to the boats in the anchorage for Halloween, but I have a feeling we won't get much if no one's ever heard of it. Besides, candy is the last thing people will have on their boats at this point after so many months of living in remote places. I wonder how you are dressed for Halloween?

I'm really sad today, Tristan. I know this sounds strange, but I'm really going to miss all of our friends. By this time next week, all the boats we arrived with will be gone. Dick and Nancy have been like my grandparents, and now I might never see them again. I know I'm going to really miss them.

The only good thing that has happened is that another boat named Thistledown *just arrived, and the people are really nice, but no kids. It seems as though most of the cruising people we meet are great.*

Dad is calling a meeting tomorrow to get our opinions on what we want to do next. We all get a chance to say what we like and dislike about this life, and any changes we want for the next trip — or if we even want to sail again. I wonder what Charlie will say. What would you say if you were me?

As promised, Dad called everyone all together early the next morning. First, the skipper spoke. "We all learned a great deal on this trip," he began. "Everyone had to learn a lot about sailing as well as all the elements of nature. We'll probably need another year to master everything we have to know. Certainly, we will never know everything about the sea or sailing, but one more year and we'll be much wiser. There are many more islands in the South Pacific to explore. I vote that we continue for one more year."

Mom now spoke up. "Before deciding," she said, "I read through some of our highlights from the journal I've been keeping. And we've been through a lot of highs and lows. Looking at the whole thing, however, I really believe that the positives outweigh the negatives. I truly miss Canada and my friends at home, but the sailing isn't out of my system, yet. I vote for at least another year."

Sam's turn was next. "I can't imagine going home to

Canada yet," he said immediately. "This adventure's too exciting. I really miss having my friends around, but we are meeting so many great people out here, I think I'd like at least another year — even if I do have to have Mom as a teacher again."

"Well, thanks for the vote of confidence," Mom laughed. "Charlie, what do you think?"

"I don't know what I want," he said slowly. "I'm kinda confused. At first I thought that I would like to become a geologist when we were in Hawaii. Then after learning about navigation, I thought that I should be an astronomer. Then I decided to be a biologist — even a marine biologist. Being a weatherman could be kind of fun too. But after seeing so many boats, I think maybe I could be a marine architect. I don't know what I want . . ."

"Hey, Charlie," answered Sam, "why don't you just become a sailor like the rest of us? Sailors have all of those jobs, you know. We did all that stuff, didn't we?"

Charlie grinned. "Yeah, we did."

So it was decided. As simple as that.